I0788410

Fae Conqueror

Tangled Fae: Book Five

Sarah K. L. Wilson

Published by Sarah K. L. Wilson, 2020.

This is a work of fiction. Similarities to real people, places, or events are entirely coincidental.

FAE CONQUEROR

First edition. May 16, 2020.

Copyright © 2020 Sarah K. L. Wilson.

Written by Sarah K. L. Wilson.

For Cale, who thoroughly owns my heart.

Other Books by Sarah K. L. Wilson

Dragon School Series
First Flight
Initiate
The Dark Prince
The Ruby Isles
Sworn
Dusk Covenant
First Message
Warring Promises
Prince of Dragons
Dark Night
Bright Hopes
Mark of Loyalty
Dire Quest
Ancient Allies
Pipe of Wings
Dragon Piper
Dust of Death
Troubled War
Starie Night
Ascendant Light
Dragon Chameleon Series
Rogue's Quest
Paths of Deception
City of Ice
Mist of Power
Silver Eyes
World of Legends
Chase the Moon
Shadow Quest

BOOK ONE

Beyond the doors, beyond the vale,
The dead, the Wild Hunt lies pale,
Who joins them now?
Who bears the shroud?
Who dies the death?
Who greets the crowd?
-Tales of the Faewald

Chapter One

I took a big breath, the magic sword quivering in my trembling hand and my mother's moaning body at my feet.

Wait, Allie. Think.

I was in this mess because I kept jumping in before thinking. This time, I needed to think. But how did you slow down and think when everything was so urgent?

My mother needed to get to the Faewald before she bled out. Maybe there, I could extract the arrow and use some of the power I had as the Balance to heal her.

But if I went now and left my father and sister in the cave, then anyone might wander by and scoop them up. And the last time that had happened, it had made everything harder.

I also had an army running loose in the woods – scattered, directionless, waiting for me. I looked up at the baby leaves sprouting in the trees. They were in this Spring forest somewhere, crashing around aimlessly.

I swallowed.

And Scouvrel was gone – stolen by the Kinslayer. Hurt – if his screams were any indication – and in need of my help.

I was only one person.

I couldn't deal with all these things at once, so I needed to prioritize.

Okay. Get my father. Get my sister – without her, I was back to the beginning of this horrible adventure. And then get back here as fast as possible to help my mother and hope that she survived until then.

"I'll be right back. Hold on," I told her, sheathing my magic sword. My path was set.

"Hunter," she moaned through clenched teeth. Her cry ripped at me.

"I'll bring him to you." I shook my head, took a big breath, and sprinted toward the cave.

The smell of my mother's stew still permeated the air, filling the Spring evening and twisting in my belly as I ran. My breath whooshed in my lungs as I tried to focus on what I was doing and not on the overwhelming wave of panic rising in me.

Scouvrel hurt and waiting for me while I chose a different priority.

Mother shot and dying.

Scouvrel might survive if I could just get to him in time.

Mother would certainly die if I didn't help her first.

The thoughts chased each other round and round, driving me mad.

I ran into the gash of rock. It took a sharp turn immediately to the left. I turned with it, scrambling over loose rocks and skinning a palm on the rock wall.

As soon as I entered the cave, the sense of hominess hit me like a punch to my belly. Someone – my mother – had spread out a rug on the floor of the cave. She'd hung clumps of dried herbs and chipped teacups on a string over a rock shelf where a breadboard and a knife waited beside a fresh loaf of bread. The stew I'd smelled bubbled and steamed on an open fire hearth. The fire vented up through a hole in the rocks in a clever way and beside the fire on a battered rocking chair, my father looked up from his whittling, his eyes bright and empty.

"Father," I gasped.

"Or rather the shell of what was once our father," my sister said wryly from her cage. It was sitting beside his rocking chair, balanced on top of my pack. My hand twitched at the sight of her so near again.

Within the cage, my sister sat, holding a walnut husk full of water. Beside her, tied to the bars with strips of cloth that matched her dress, sat Queen Anabetha with a narrow-eyed grimace painting her face.

I barely choked back a gasp.

They were both battered and rough-looking – which did nothing to hide their ferocity and hatred. My sister had a burn across one cheek and Anabetha had a bloody bandage slung across one eye. They'd fought – obviously. And it looked like my sister had won. Had my mother known?

"Sister," I said warily.

"Where is our mother?" she asked. "Or has your stupidity gotten her killed?"

I flinched at her words, but they drew me back to reality. I needed to focus. I pulled up my blindfold, ignoring the spirit world as I tried to concentrate on the physical.

I snatched up the cage and gathered up my pack from under it. I opened the top of the pack, checking to see if anything was missing. The key sparkled in the light of the fire and I pulled it out and put it in my jacket pocket before picking up my pack. My sister's eyes watched my every move with hungry desire. Did she realize that key could open her cage?

I closed the pack, slinging it over my shoulder. My mother and father's cloaks were hung on jagged edges of rock near the fire. I grabbed them. We'd need them.

"Hunter," I said gently to my father. "I need your help. Genda is in trouble."

"Genda?" he asked worriedly, searching my eyes as if he was trying to remember me. He was far too young for this – barely forty.

I swallowed down a lump of emotion.

"Yes. Here, put on your cloak." I helped him with the cloak, my eyes flicking around the room. Was there anything else we needed?

I hurried to a pallet at one side of the cave and grabbed two blankets. One to make a litter for my mother and one for bandages.

Water.

There was a half-full barrel beside a waterskin. I filled the waterskin quickly and shoved it into my father's hands with the blankets.

"Please carry these."

He nodded numbly and I barely bit back a snarl of frustration at how fate had left him a shell of his old self. At one time, he would have led this expedition to save my mother.

I tied the cage to my belt. Something pinched my skin and this time I did snarl.

"Behave in there, or I'll put you in the fire."

"You won't," my sister said. It was weird to hear her voice while she was invisible to me. "You need me. You know that now."

I ignored her, grabbing my father's arm and guiding him out of the cave. There had been no weapons. No way to arm him. Would he even remember how to use a bow?

I pulled him along behind me, hurrying to where my mother lay gasping on the rocks.

"Genda!" He dropped the blankets when he saw her, scrambling to her side.

"We need two poles to use for a litter," I said smoothly, striding into the trees nearby and drawing my belt knife to quickly cut and strip a pair of poplar saplings. They would do.

I marched back to where my father sat, crying beside my mother, grabbed one of the blankets, and tied it to the poles to form a rough litter. We'd carry her on that.

"You're wasting your time," my sister said. "You can't save her now."

"Not here," I agreed.

"Not anywhere. She's dying."

My blindfold slipped as I finished with the blanket and my spirit gaze met Anabetha's single eye. She looked from Hulanna to me and back again.

"She doesn't look much like you, Lady of Cups."

"It hardly matters what she looks like," Hulanna said haughtily. "All that matters is if she dies in the right place at the right time. She must die at the Dread Door. And soon."

"You should know this, sister of the Lady of Cups." Queen Anabetha's voice was menacing. "I will get free of this cage and when I do, I will skin you and make you dance for me without your skin."

I shivered. I should be getting used to people wanting to see me dead, but somehow, I just never did.

"If you think my sister is fierce," I shot back, "you haven't seen what I can do to Fae. Just keep threatening me and see how that turns out for you."

I pulled my blindfold back up and tore a strip of cloth from the second blanket, wadding it around the arrow in my mother's chest and trying to tie it in place so that it didn't move when we moved her to the pallet. I laid her cloak over her. She'd passed out, but she was still breathing.

"Are you a healing woman?" my father asked me.

"No, I'm just trying to help," I said gently.

He nodded, his lips twisting as he fought tears.

"This is a bad hit. It's hard to survive a shot like this," he said.

"Yes," I agreed. "Now, help me get her on this litter."

He moved in place to help me.

I shook my head. It shouldn't be me treating my father like a child and trying not to overwhelm him. It should be him protecting me. But life didn't always work that way, did it? I'd seen old men and women in the village lose their minds and have to be cared for by their grown children – fed porridge by the fire, cleaned by the very hands and arms they'd birthed into this world. But that had all felt like something a long way away – something that was someone else's problem. I hadn't expected it to be me talking gently to someone who once was the strongest, wisest person I'd known.

My mother's eyes opened, and she groaned as we moved her to the litter.

"Where to?" my father asked.

"Another world." I drew my sword from the scabbard and sliced the air with the thought of my mother and how she needed help. As soon as the tear in the air formed, I gestured to my father to pick up his end of the litter as I lifted mine. Together, we slowly raised my mother into the air. She was breathing sharply through her mouth, gasping and hissing with every breath.

With a shudder, I stepped through the rip in the air and into the Faewald.

This had better work. It had just better work.

Chapter Two

It was day in the Faewald.

Thank goodness for that. I couldn't deal with any Blood Moons or Wild Hunts right now.

We stepped into the white light of the Faewald day and I stumbled as the horror of it hit me in the chest. For a moment, I felt as though I couldn't breathe.

I'd forgotten to pull down my blindfold. Somehow, the Faewald seemed worse than ever.

It tangled and twisted, seeming to move like a beetle under a cloth. The very ground writhed and wove under my feet, making my vision wobble in a way that immediately filled me with nausea. I choked back bile as I stumbled forward. I couldn't put the litter down until my father was through with the other end. I tried to scrape my cheek against my shoulder to pull down the blindfold but all I succeeded in doing was making myself dizzier.

We had emerged directly in front of the Dread Door – or so I thought. From here, the doors looked like they were woven of writhing snakes. Blinding light shot through the cracks and around the edges.

My heart sank. I hated that door with everything in me. If it wasn't for the Dread Door, half the people I knew wouldn't be trying to kill me.

My father stumbled through the tear with a terrified cry and I managed to gasp out, "Help me lower her."

We lowered the litter to the smooth stone, and I swallowed down the memory of Scouvrel kneeling right here just days ago, looking at me with eyes wide and full of longing. If I stood here and jammed a knife through my own throat, nothing would make him happier, right? The thought of it turned my stomach.

I shook my head as my mother settled, moaning onto the stone and I could finally reach up and rip my blindfold down.

I sucked in a deep, relieved breath at the same time that my father seemed to fall in on himself, sinking to the stone, wrapping his arms around his head and sobbing.

"This place! This terrible place! What have you done in taking us here?"

"It's her only hope," I muttered.

"Genda, my Genda," his whisper was hard to hear through his sobs. "I didn't mean to bring you here. I'm so sorry. Please, please don't die. I love you."

He was a broken man, clutching his dying wife with gnarled hands and a broken mind.

And now I was crying. Which was such a colossal waste of time. I swiped my tears from my eyes.

"You're all ridiculous," my sister swore. "A disgrace to our family name. And you wonder why I left? You wonder why I wanted more? This is why. You pathetic creatures are why!"

I knocked her cage with an angry snort. Let them feel the burn of those bars! Anabetha shrieked but my sister was resolutely silent. I ripped the cage from my belt and tossed it to the side. I would deal with them later.

I crawled over to my mother across the blood-stained stone in front of the doors. It was shockingly smooth – untouched by the prolific carvings on the door.

My mother panted, her hands trembling at her sides. Her face had gone a ghastly pale and her brow was slick with sweat.

"Alastra," she breathed as she saw me.

"I'm doing what I can," I said, tightly, my hands hovering over her.

Where was my magic? Where was the power of the Balance? I should be able to feel it. Then I could heal her and just balance it with something else. Maybe it would want someone killed in exchange for my mother's life. I didn't even care if that was the price. I had two possible victims in my cage.

Beside me, my father rocked back and forth, little cries of horror ripping from his throat punctuating the rocking. This place was death to him.

"Don't let murder stain you," my mother gasped. Her hand reached up and rested on my waist for a moment as if she was trying to draw me into a hug, but her hand dragged along my jacket and then fell away.

"Mother, hold on," I said tightly. "I'm working on a way to heal you."

"Genda, my love, my sweet love," my father moaned, his arms still wrapped around his head. "I can't go out. The roots will tangle me up."

I swallowed against the rough lump in my throat.

"Bring your father to the Spring of Tears," my mother gasped through gritted teeth. "Promise me."

"Of course," I said, as I looked at the arrow planted in her chest. Balance. If I took the arrow out and healed it, perhaps the magic would work if I agreed to put the arrow in someone else's chest.

"No, Allie," she grabbed my shirt with surprising strength. I met her eyes, surprised by the sudden burst of life in them. "You must *promise* me to take your father to the Spring of Tears."

"I promise," I said, stunned. "Rest now. I will find a way to heal you."

She ignored that. "If you don't take him there, it will have been for nothing. It's only the two of us. I've loved him so much."

She must find his insanity as troubling as I did. Maybe worse. Of course this was her last wish. I just wished I could help her live and let her have hundreds of wishes. I smoothed her sweaty brow with a hand.

"Of course, mother. I love you, too. And I love him."

She nodded, her face pained but her expression satisfied at the same time. "Good. Good. You'll be a parent someday and then you'll understand."

I already understood responsibility. I didn't need to be a parent to understand that.

"I love you and your sister so much," my mother said, her voice weak. "I'm sorry that I didn't tell you more sooner. I forgot it. I blocked it out. And by the time the memories came back, it was too late. Too late to help you."

I risked a glance at my sister. Her face was cold and unreadable.

"I love you, too," I said, sniffing as I tried to hold back tears. A single tear escaped my grasp, slipping down and dropping to darken my mother's dress. "I don't care if you forgot things."

"Remember that. Whatever else … just remember that I love you." Her eyes were growing unfocused. She searched for my father. "Hunter?"

"Genda, my Genda," my father said, still rocking back and forth, terror stretching his face into a mask.

My mother reached a hand to touch him.

"Love you forever, my Hunter. My brave, sweet man." She was saying her goodbyes.

"Please don't die," I whispered, embarrassed by my weakness in the face of this. I just wanted her to be okay. I just wanted to walk into our house and see her there smiling again with a big pot of hot soup and a freshly scrubbed floor.

"Some things have to be."

I thought she was going to close her eyes and slip away then. I bit my lip, preparing for the worst.

She surprised me.

Her hand reached up and gripped my own one last time and then with a cry that sounded more like a war-cry than anything else, she shoved me aside and turned over, rising on all fours as blood poured from her arrow wound. She forced herself to her feet so quickly that I was still scrambling to mine as she took a staggering step forward. She kissed my father's brow on her way past, and then, still bleeding badly, she stumbled to the Dread Door.

Something gleamed in her hand.

The key.

She'd taken it from my pocket when I thought she was trying to embrace me.

I opened my mouth to speak, stumbling forward, but the key was already in the tangled lock and with a squeal like the dead being wrenched from their graves, she cracked open the door, took one last affectionate look over her shoulder at me, and wrenched the door open.

Bright light seared across my vision in waving tentacles of light, it burned my eyes and filled my brain with pain. It felt almost alive – as if a many-armed creature lay behind that door, made entirely of light. And that light was hungry to snatch us up. I fell to my knees, blinking against the purple after-light behind my eyelids.

By the time the purple after-images were clear enough to see, the door was closed, the light had faded, and my mother was gone.

Later in the Faewald ...

~~Sing for the Hunter strong and brave!~~
Sing for her mother, bright and glorious!
Sing, sing, for a song ~~they~~ she deserves!
Sing for the great sacrifice of the mother ~~and the stalwart loyalty of the daughter~~!
Sing for the Faewald that was and will be again!
-Tales of the Faewald

Chapter Three

I stumbled to the door, grasping for the golden key.

"I wouldn't if I were you," a voice said from inside the cage.

I looked back to see Queen Anabetha smirking at me from the cage.

She was alone.

"Where is my sister?" I asked, feeling suddenly light-headed.

"If you go through the doors, you don't get to come back," Anabetha said grandly. "The other side of those doors is death. Do you believe in an afterlife?"

"Of course," I said, but I wasn't paying attention, I was searching for my sister. How could she have gotten free? My head was spinning.

Behind me, my father's sobs were all I could hear.

"That's what's on the other side of the door," Anabetha said. "The Beyond. The Afterlife. The Judgment."

I looked at her, stunned. "You believe in judgment?"

"Everyone is judged," she said with narrowed eyes that looked like she was judging me right now. "That's a universal truth."

"Then why don't you live better?" I demanded. I drew the key from the door with a trembling hand and shoved it in my pocket.

"Why don't you?"

Why *didn't* I live better? Because I didn't know how to do better than I was doing. That was why. Because even when I did want to do better, I found myself slipping back to this. Because this awful mess was my very best.

I leaned my forehead against the Dread Door.

"Why did you go? What were you thinking?" I asked aloud. But there would be no answers from my mother.

There was the sound of soft feet on the rock behind me – whisper-quiet beneath my father's sobs.

"I would think that you of all people would understand that ... Balance."

I spun to look at the speaker.

The Sooth seemed to tremble in the wind, her white hair blowing behind her and her antlers bright in the white light of the Faewald. Her eyes, I realized, were exactly like a barn cat's.

"Sooth," I gasped.

"Your prisoner is correct. You should not go through those doors unless you want all this to end."

"My mother," I said vaguely, gesturing at the door.

"I saw that. Such an interesting development." The Sooth smiled and I found I didn't like her smile at all.

"I thought you were supposed to bring enlightenment and clarity," I said frostily. "But you just seem to show up like a raven – whenever something is dead."

A dark cloud passed overhead and suddenly – as if he had materialized out of nowhere – her stag was there behind her, snorting and pawing at the ground with his frosty hoof, the spider webs tangled in his antlers fluttered in a breeze I couldn't feel. The Faewald felt colder, suddenly.

"That's how fairy godmothers work," she said.

I scoffed. "You don't believe those stories, do you? I have yet to meet a Fae who wanted to do something nice for a human."

"Is that so?" the Sooth raised an eyebrow as if she didn't believe me.

"Yes." I bit the word off at the end.

"I'm the fairy godmother," she said with a self-satisfied smile. "The one in *every* story. When I find myself near mortals, I see their futures and I tell them what I can."

"How adorable," I said, adopting one of Scouvrel's disdainful looks. "Did you see my sister when you arrived? I seem to have lost her. Or did you magic her away with a flick of your wand?"

"Your mother set her free when she went willingly through the doors. Did you fail to realize that? You won't find the Lady of Cups here. She's back in the mortal world now. Haven't you heard the story of the Substitute? A mother's love is a powerful thing," the Sooth said, as if it was obvious. "But I wanted to talk to you about futures."

"What?" I asked stunned. "She's free because of my mother?"

The Sooth shrugged, her stooped shoulders looking delicate as she moved them. Had she always looked so fragile? "You're the Balance. Surely you must have felt the transaction. One goes free when the other dies."

I felt my mouth fall open.

She shrugged again. "But since you are speechless, I will speak of futures. You have one. A possible future that starts right now. I see three possibilities."

"What, no riddles?" I asked wryly.

"Would you prefer riddles?" Her tone was so hard it could have chipped glass.

"No."

She stared at me and it was all I could do not to look away before she finally continued with an irritated burr in her voice.

"In one possibility, you return to the mortal world and when I next see yourself, you call yourself Oolag and ride at your sister's side. You rule the mortal half of the world while she rules the Faewald and Vhalot is now the Knave. In the next future, you go to the home of the Kinslayer and when next I see you, you are on this stone slab, punching a dagger through your own heart. You seem to be enjoying it." I shivered but she kept speaking. "And in the third, you go to the Spring of Tears and you offer your tears to the Spring and when next I see you, you are conquering the Faewald with the Knave by your side."

"And then?"

She shook her head. "And then I don't know. But you must choose the best possibility of the three."

"Which would you choose?" I asked wryly.

"The one where you go to the Spring of Tears."

I raised a doubtful eyebrow. "Even though that one leads to me conquering your realm?"

"Well, in that future the world continues, so that seems like the best one," her tone was nearly as snippy as mine had been.

She turned around and was walking away before I could close my jaw with a snap.

"Sooth?" I called. "Sooth!"

But she faded into a mist I hadn't realized was there.

With an annoyed sound in the back of my throat, I gathered up Queen Anabetha's cage and tied it to my belt. So much for fairy godmothers. They were the worst. I could see why they got the girls in the stories into so much trouble.

"You could release me, you know," Queen Anabetha said.

"And what? Will you promise not to harm me?" I asked.

"No."

"Promise not to kill me?" I asked, but I was still looking into the mist, trying to catch a glimpse of the Sooth. There had to be more to that prophesy – right?

"No."

"Promise not to turn on me immediately?"

"Definitely not," she said.

"Then I don't know why you think I'd give you anything," I said, giving up on the Sooth and walking over to my father. I gently put a hand on his shoulder.

"Genda?" he asked, looking up.

"I need you to follow me, Hunter. We need to go somewhere – somewhere that Genda asked us to go."

"Where?" he asked simply, his eyes on me were like a little child's. It made me feel ill.

"The Spring of Tears," I said. "And I know just who can show us the way."

Chapter Four

"I am *not* a lantern!" Queen Anabetha protested from her seat in the cage – but that didn't prevent me from holding her up high like she was lighting our path. I'd cut her bonds and given her some of the fabric from the litter to protect herself from the iron bars, but I still needed her to guide me through the Faewald.

"Bargain with me, Queen Anabetha," I said, trying my best to use Scouvrel's cunning charm.

"I don't bargain with mortals." She stood grandly as if she still thought she was Queen. Maybe she would be if I brought her back. Maybe she would stand tall and proud and stride back into the mortal camp and they would flock to her with gratitude. But would they do that if they knew what she was?

"You are my captive," I said clearly as I led my father along a wide road – the only road that led from the Dread Door. I didn't know where it went – but I had to go somewhere.

Maybe I should use the sword to go back to the Mortal Realm and then just think of the Spring of Tears before I came back to the Faewald. But I would have no way to prevent the passage of time and I could lose decades doing that. My army might have already been defeated in the Mortal Realm. Scouvrel might already be dead here. The Faewald made everything tenuous, dangerous, and unpredictable.

"You can't leave that cage unless I let you out," I told Anabetha. "And when you leave, where will you go? Will you return to the Mortal Realm? Will you try to be a Queen there again? What will Sir Eckelmeyer and the other knights say when I tell them you are Fae?"

"They won't believe you," she said smugly. "You're nothing but property – the wife of Sir Eckelmeyer."

"I'm more than property," I said, holding the cage up to my face. I stopped on the road. "But, if you are of no use to me, then there's no point dragging you around. You're dead weight. I'll just go back to the door, open it, and toss the cage in there."

Her glamor flickered and for a moment she was nothing but a terrified child, huddled away from the iron bars with huge eyes and a foxy face. Her scraps of armor clung to her like the last leaves on a winter tree.

"Your sister said you were the good one."

"And my sister doesn't lie, because she is Fae," I said grimly. "You don't know what 'good' is, Anabetha. 'Good' is me purging the earth of someone like you."

"What do you know about me? What gives you the right to judge?" She lifted her chin – every inch the queen.

"Being the Balance gives me the right to judge," I said, lifting an eyebrow, and I felt the weight of that settle over me, as if this acceptance mixed with passing judgment had settled the role on my shoulders in a way it never had been before. "I used to think before that I didn't need to accept the role of the Balance. I was wrong. What I needed to do was to learn how to turn it to suit my purposes. And I'm a quick learner."

She swallowed, fear filling her face, and then her shoulders slumped, and she nodded. "What do you want?"

"I want you to guide me to the Spring of Tears by the quickest method possible that will still get us all there alive and unharmed. Once there, I want you to help me use it to restore the mind of my father."

We both glanced at where he stood, his fingernails digging into his cheeks, leaving long red tears in the skin as he tried to slowly rip his own face off. Grimly, I reached over and gently took one of his hands.

"In return," Anabetha said. "You will set out to the Spring of Tears immediately, without stopping to fulfill a different goal or purpose. You will not delay or attempt to change this bargain. You will release me immediately upon the restoration of your father's mind and you will not reveal my identity outside the Faewald."

"It is agreed between you and me," I said grimly.

"It is agreed," Anabetha said, her tiny face equally grim. "In that case, you're going the wrong way."

"This is the only road." I pointed at it, as if to elaborate but she only shrugged.

"You agreed not to delay."

I nodded. "Fine. Show me the better way."

"Turn here," she said, pointing off the road and into the thick grass nearby. "Follow the grass up to the rise."

I drew my father along behind me, keeping hold of his hand. His eyes were on everything except me, his lips trembling at what he saw and sweat trickling down his temple. No wonder this place had driven him mad. I shouldn't have brought him here – even if I had no other choice.

The shoulders of his shirt were damp. I pulled the shoulder back on one side and gasped. His wounds there were opening again.

"She nailed me to a tree," he said, his eyes wide when they met mine. "Stole my pain to feed her."

"That's over now, Hunter," I said gently. But I was worried about those wounds.

I was also worried about his mind. This place was breaking him down worse than ever. By the time we reached the top of the rise, he was muttering to himself a constant, "Genda. Genda. Genda."

Every time he said my mother's name, it pierced my heart. Why had she done it? I could have saved her. We could have saved my father together. There could have been a happy ending for us. If she'd just held on ...

"See that pod?" Anabetha asked suddenly.

There was a long vine growing on the top of the hill and things that looked like green beans the size of an adult human grew out of the pod. One of them had blossomed into a purple flower, but there was something wrong about it – where there should have been a pistil and stamen, there was only a dark hole.

The darkness felt wrong – oily, inky in a way I couldn't describe.

"Walk into the flower," Anabetha said and her eyes were far too bright.

"I don't think that's a good idea," I said reluctantly. "Scouvrel never took me through any flowers."

"The bargain said the fastest way," Anabetha said coolly. "This is the fastest way that I know. You know that you cannot break a bargain, Balance."

I felt a hot tug in my chest. She wasn't wrong. I couldn't break this agreement – not even if I wanted to. I took a step forward, and with a sigh, I reached back, took my father's hand, and stepped into the dark opening of the flower.

"No, please no!" *The girl moaning looked just like Anabetha – pretty, delicate, her huge eyes pleading for mercy.*

I tried to look away, but it was not me controlling my body but someone else. That someone was laughing as she forced a vial to the crying girl's lips and made her drink.

"I will make a better queen than you ever would."

I stumbled through the darkness and out the trembling papery petals of a huge blue flower. I couldn't stop shaking.

I had murdered that girl.

No, not me. Queen Anabetha. Malentric. The Fae in my cage.

"You killed her," I gasped. "You killed her and took her place."

The Fae in the cage looked ill. She swallowed and then gasped as if she might vomit.

"Well, now you know why your precious Scouvrel didn't take you through the Nightshades. They show you memories. Secrets. The secrets of those you journey with."

"And if you journey by yourself?" I asked, but mostly to buy time. I was watching my father watch me. He blinked, owlishly, and then shook his head as if he didn't believe something.

"Then you see your own secrets – which might be even worse. The things we hide from ourselves are hidden for a reason," she said with a laugh.

Chapter Five

None of this was funny.

I turned around slowly, trying to assess where we were. I didn't see a spring, though I did see another hill in the distance – a hill with more pods and what appeared to be a gathering of Fae eating around a table. The bright colors of the grass and flowers surrounding them made this feel more like a story than a real scene.

"You didn't take me to the Spring, Anabetha."

"That's *Queen* Anabetha. And you didn't expect to get there in one step, did you?" she asked wryly. "It will be at least three or four hops by way of the Nightshade. Now, climb on up that hill, and let's try again. This appears to be the Cumberbarrows and from here it shouldn't be too far to the Spring of Tears. Maybe we'll get lucky and the next Nightshade will take us there in a single hop."

"Lucky?" I asked through clenched teeth. I should have been more careful in my bargaining. With a growl, I led my father from one hill to the next. The feasting Fae made me nervous. Fae weren't usually outside in the day. They were usually asleep.

"Do you think my sister went through the door with my mother?" I asked Anabetha. It still worried me that I didn't know what had happened to her. Could I trust the Sooth who said that she had somehow gone back to the mortal world?

Queen Anabetha laughed nastily. "Obviously not. But your mother's suicide clearly freed her from your power. Isn't that interesting? Who would have thought she would be desperate enough to die just to free her daughter from you? I'm starting to understand why you killed for a role. You fill it completely."

I ignored her cutting words. I hadn't chosen this – it had been thrust upon me. And I didn't believe my mother had meant to kill herself ... did I?

As we climbed the hill and drew closer, I realized that the people sitting at the banquet weren't alive. They were made of stone, frozen in place with cups of tea raised halfway to their lips and saucers held in their hands as if they had been enjoying a delightful feast before freezing in time.

Vines wrapped around the table, curling around the people and tangling in the food – which still looked as edible and delightful as ever. The strawberry cake with clotted cream made my mouth water even though I could see a hand holding a fork with a bit of it on the end of the fork – and while the cake was still bright and fresh the hand was entirely swallowed up in white mold, the arm thick with moss that crawled up onto the shoulders and hat. Tiny blue flowers speckled the top of the hat, reaching for the pale Faewald sun.

My father reached for a spiraled roll that smelled strongly of butter and cinnamon, but I snatched his hand away before he could put the food in his open mouth.

"Don't eat it," I told him. "There's a reason these Fae are stone now."

"Balance," said the Queen in the cage. And as she said the words, I could feel it in the air. For life stolen from the delectable food, their lives had been stolen. But why? There had to be more to it than that.

I shook my head. The last Balance must have done this. I could still feel it in the air – a sense of rightness that came from finding balance. I didn't like it that I could feel that. I liked it even less that it seemed to satisfy me. Whatever these Fae had done, their punishment had fit somehow and the Balance inside me reveled in that.

I shivered.

"We need to keep going," I said, angling for the Nightshade ahead, but before I took the last step into the flower, I hesitated. What would I see if I went down this road again? Was I brave enough to face it?

I stepped into the flower, clutching my father's hand and hoping for the best.

What I saw was my mother's face. My heart twisted at the sight of it. She was looking in my eyes with concern in hers.

"Hunter? Can you hear me? Do you know what you just said?" She looked around furtively. "Don't say it again. Goodie Chanter is a good woman, but if she hears ... if she knows what I'm planning ... Just keep it between us, Chanter. Our little secret, okay?"

"I wish I'd remembered sooner. I could have prevented all of this." She seemed to be crying as she looked around one more time and then leaned her forehead to mine. "I still love my daughter. No matter what anyone says, blood is blood. I'll do what I need to do to protect her. And so will you, dear. So will you."

I stepped from the flower with a gasp. My mother. Just seeing her face again felt like a knife twisting inside me. She shouldn't be dead. She shouldn't be.

I fought a tremble in my lips.

I was so overwhelmed by feeling that I hardly noticed the sun going down in the distance and the moon rising – still a Blood Moon but now full to the brim with bright red blood.

Just beyond us, someone was speaking. "Tonight. That's right."

I needed to keep out of their sight. Any Fae who saw me might try to kill me to claim my new role. I couldn't hear the other speaker, but then the first was speaking again.

"A Spectacle! All the Faewald will be there." There was a pause. "Yes." Another pause. "Yes. The Knave. That's what I'm telling you! The Kinslayer will put him on display." There was snickering. "Well, he can't *kill* him, but there are things worse than death. We have to hurry. I'm thinking of taking the Nightshades to get there quickly. This will be the Spectacle of a lifetime!"

My hand flew up and covered my mouth.

Scouvrel.

He was still alive.

My heart ached with the thought of it.

Alive and in trouble.

I needed to go to him. I needed to get him before this "Spectacle" could happen.

From the cage, Anabetha whispered to me, "I hope you're not getting any ideas about seeing Spectacles, Balance. You made a bargain with me. And the moon is rising. The Wild Hunt will begin any moment now."

But so what if I had a bargain with her? I wasn't bound to honor it the way that the Fae were. Scouvrel was my husband ...

and my friend. My heart ached at the thought of leaving him to the Kinslayer. He needed me.

I took a step back toward the Nightshade.

"We are close to the Spring," Anabetha whispered. "One more crossing."

We could always come back to the Spring later. I took a second step back and something clamped over my heart. It felt like I could hardly breathe. I choked, gasping for air, little lights dancing across my vision. I tried to take another step back and my foot froze in place.

"You can't break your promise to me," Anabetha hissed. "See? It holds. It binds you."

I stepped forward again and my breath came back. I heaved in a long, trembling breath.

"Are you hurt, miss?" my father asked shyly. "Hold my hand and I will keep you safe from this hellish place."

"I'm all right," I said, taking his hand again.

And then the horns of the hunt sounded, and I sprang into a run without knowing where to go or what to do. All I knew, was that Allie Hunter wasn't going to turn to stone out in the fields from being too scared to run. Not Allie. There would be no saving Scouvrel now – I had to obey the bargain, and that meant I had to run.

I dragged my father along behind me.

There was another Nightshade nearby. I plunged through without thinking about the consequences.

I was somewhere underground looking at broken, dirty men. Men wearing something that looked like tabards. Knights.

"How long will you keep them here?" a nearby voice asked.

I recognized my voice as Queen Anabetha's. "As long as I like. After all, they tried to rebel against me. My own knights! They'll find that others will rally to me. And they'll hear about it from you day after day as they slowly rot in my cellars while I live only a floor above them, enjoying the life they'll never have again."

I stumbled from the flower, shivering from head to foot. Any sympathy I might have ever had for Anabetha was long gone.

I took a long breath to steady myself and looked around, letting my father catch his breath. His eyes were squeezed shut against the pain of whatever he'd seen. It was still night, and in the distance, the horns were sounding, but in front of us, a spring tinkled and trickled, its diamond water flashing under the red of the Blood Moon. In the center of the spring, a tree with red leaves stood tall and proud. The winds that shook it blew leaves off the tree so that they drifted down and blanketed the spring with crimson red. It reminded me too much of my mother's blood dripping from her arrow wound. I shuddered.

But we'd made it. This was the Spring of Tears.

Chapter Six

The horns of the Wild Hunt sounded in the distance and I turned in a circle, looking for a dwelling. Any dwelling. The Hunt would be upon us soon.

"Are you blind?" Anabetha asked with a curse as I turned in a circle a second time. "The Spring is right there! We've made it!"

"The Hunt," I gasped.

"They won't chase you to the *tree*. No one in their right mind will go there - not even the Hunt. Once you reach the tree you have to solve the riddle."

"Riddle?"

She rolled her eyes. "Someone needs to kill you. Quickly. You are too stupid to be one of the four."

I growled under my breath and looked to my father. "Can you swim, Hunter?"

"Yes," he said simply but his gaze was far away.

I nodded and led him to the edge of the water but when I looked in, I gasped. My mother's face was staring out at me. I bit my lip so hard that I tasted blood. My father fell to his knees.

"Genda. My Genda."

The Fae queen kept her eyes upward, as if she didn't dare look at the surface of the water.

So, it wasn't real. It was yet another torture of the Faewald. My mother smiled at me as if she agreed. But this illusion was too accurate. The tremulous smile on my mother's face felt as real as the frown on mine. My breath hitched at the sight of it.

My eyes were welling up. No, I couldn't do this right now. I scrubbed my eyes with the back of my sleeve. There would be time for grief later when threats were past, and all this was over. Later.

"Come on," I said to my father, tugging at his hand, but he shook his head, refusing. "You need to come with me, Hunter."

His gaze was stuck to the surface of the water.

"Hunter?"

Still, he didn't look at me. He just kept shaking his head.

"You have to come with me."

In the distance, I heard the howls of the hunt. Fear shot through me, making my guts feel like water.

They had Scouvrel. They were coming for me. We were running out of time.

I stepped into the water and as if I had broken a spell, my father shrieked, leaping toward me, arms outstretched. We fell into the water together, and it was all I could do to spin and shove his hands away as they reached for my neck.

I surfaced, trying to gasp for air, but before I had a full breath, a hand tangled in my hair, plunging me under the surface.

Bubbles broke from my mouth, racing to the surface.

No! Not like this! This wasn't how I died!

My father was insane. He didn't mean this. It was a mistake.

My heart hammered in my chest as I grappled against him, but he was bigger than me – stronger than me.

I'd lost the cage.

My pack was dragging me down.

What else did I have?

I pulled my belt knife out and jabbed at his arm. His grip loosened enough that I could dodge back, fighting to get my legs under me enough to stand. My left leg wobbled, digging into the boggy mud at the bottom of the pond. I fought for balance.

There! My head broke the surface and I dragged in a long breath.

"Father!" I called, barely ducking under a clumsy attack as he barrelled toward me. "Stop!"

This time his swipe was so close that I was knocked off balance. I plunged beneath the water.

I couldn't win – not like this. He was bigger than me. He wasn't able to listen to reason. I had to fight back, or I would die at his hand and he'd be doomed to live insane forever in a land that terrified him.

I gritted my teeth with determination and sheathed my belt knife, pulling the axe handle from my belt instead. I came up swinging, and my luck held.

The axe handle struck my father across the head, the hit reverberating painfully down my arms and shoulders. He clutched his head, moaning.

His pain stung me, but I pushed those emotions aside and grabbed him by the collar, tugging him toward the tree. He followed me, dazed. I'd already gone a step before I remembered.

The cage!

Floundering in the water, I felt with both hands looking for it. There!

I snatched the cage up into the air, watching anxiously as the water poured from between the bars leaving a sodden Anabetha collapsed on the floor.

Be alive, be alive! I didn't have time to wait and see if she was.

I grabbed my father's collar again and dragged him through the waist-high water of the Spring of Tears. I struggled toward where the red-leaved branches plunged into the water.

We pushed past them into the shadowed water beyond. Dappled and dark, the water on the other side seemed different – cold, sharper, sadder, and alive in a way that the water outside the veil of red leaves had been.

At the base of the tree was just enough tufted grass to find dry land. I hauled my father and Anabetha up onto the grass and left them there as I tried to catch my breath. My father lay on the grass, clutching his head, his breathing weak.

Had I killed him? Was he dying even now?

I lifted the axe handle, swiped it through the air, and let the spirit light illuminate this strange, dark place. The tree was very old – its trunk as wide around as a small cottage. Its bark was smooth white, those odd, curving branches hung like curtains on every side. The eerie red light of the Blood Moon barely penetrated the branches and I was glad for the light of my spirit torch.

My father took up most of the grassy tuft – which I realized was a tangle of tree roots. There was only enough room beside him for the cage. Inside the cage, a sodden Anabetha was rising to her feet, choking and gasping. She vomited loudly, wiping her mouth with the back of her hand.

"You'll pay for this, mortal. You almost killed me," she wheezed, but I was too busy staring at the tree trunk to worry about her.

Something was written on it – scored into the bark so deeply that even time and weathering had not erased the words. I squinted at them and as if by magic they seemed to morph into something I could read.

Tears of love, tears of despair, will feed the tree and fill the spring.

They bind and heal, restore to health, and change what time will bring.

But only if you pay the price and take pain to your breast.
Nothing comes from nothing, not healing and not rest.
Speak the name in your heart and lay it bare,
Risk the love of your life and the future you share.
Or choose to sit five years in silence beneath this tree.
Either pain we'll take, in exchange for what you wish to be.
But only one chance you'll have to decide,
So make your choice count and enjoy the ride.

"It's not much of a riddle," I said dryly. "It says right out what it offers and what it demands."

"Is it asking you to relinquish your crown?" Queen Anabetha asked, squeezing out her wet dress. It hung around her like an old curtain.

"I don't have a crown," I said sourly. I didn't have five years to spare, either. I hardly had five minutes.

"Is it offering you your freedom?" she asked, her voice almost faint.

"Hardly," I said, sparing a glance for my father.

My mother said his sanity was key. But both these prices were steep. I didn't dare risk five years of my life. Not with Scouvrel in trouble and not with my army running blindly around the Mortal Court or my sister out there somewhere, likely trying to get back to her army. On the other hand, if I said Scouvrel's real name aloud, I really did risk him – his free will and his very life. Because Queen Anabetha would hear me say it. And anyone else here might hear it, too.

"Then," Anabetha said. "I think it's obvious. The tree has a different message for each person and the riddle is trying to find the loophole."

"There is no loophole," I said as I read the words again. There was only one name on my heart.

I swallowed. My only hope was to free Queen Anabetha before she heard the name, too. But if I did that, then she might attack me before I could even heal my father's mind.

I reached for the cage at the same moment that she said, "You can't do anything else before you answer the riddle, or else you won't get another opportunity. You must be steadfast."

"What?" I said.

Her voice sounded desperate. "If you were planning to drown me, don't. If you do anything – go anywhere – you'll lose your chance. There's only one chance. You read that part, didn't you? Neither of us will get another chance if you do anything."

"I was going to free you," I said.

She closed her eyes as if she was making a decision. This was her chance, too.

I swallowed and looked at the tree. I needed my father's mind back. I had promised my mother I would get it back. Besides – I loved him. I hated that he was like this. But did I dare speak Scouvrel's name aloud? In front of an enemy?

"Scouvrel," I said, hoping that alone would be enough.

In the cage, Anabetha laughed.

I felt cold sweat breaking out over me. My father moaned and rose to his hands and knees.

"Genda," he begged. "Please don't go."

My eyes stung as I looked from the faerie in the cage and back to the tree and then back to my father.

I had to take the risk.

"Finmark Thorne," I whispered.

Anabetha began to laugh and then she said – quick as a whip – "Hulanna Hunter."

Light flared with a flash of purple light.

I blinked, rubbing my eyes, and inside my heart was sinking.

I shouldn't have done that. I really shouldn't have.

When I could see again, Anabetha was gone.

No! No! No!

That meant the clock was ticking. If Anabetha was gone, then she was on her way back to her army. And if Hulanna wasn't dead, then she was on her way back to hers. And that meant I needed to get to the mortal world immediately to stop them both before it was too late.

And if she found Scouvrel on the way, then she would know his name and be able to command him to do anything she wanted.

Cold sweat broke out on my brow and my belly twisted painfully. I shouldn't have spoken his name aloud. It wasn't a secret for me to tell.

I picked up the empty cage with trembling hands, tied it to my belt, and looked up. My father's gaze met mine, horror in his eyes.

"Allie?" he asked. "Is that really you?"

Chapter Seven

"**F**ather!" my cry was half-strangled as I reached for him. His embrace was warm and solid – the embrace of a father, a protector. "It's you."

He drew back, running a hand through his hair nervously. "I'm back in this place. I don't like it, Allie."

One of his hands wandered to his shoulder – where a wound had been from Hulanna nailing him to a tree. It wasn't seeping through his shirt anymore, but he shuddered at the touch.

"You know who I am," I said in wonder.

"Of course," he looked offended by that. His brow crinkled as he peered at me. "You're my Allie. My daughter. Though your eyes are two colors now – green and brown and on the brown-eyed side of your face your freckles have gone white against the tan of your skin."

They had? I was becoming more the Balance every day.

"But what else do you know?" I asked softly. Tears threatened just outside my control. If I had to tell him about Hulanna … about mother.

Wrinkles formed on his brow and then a dawning realization. I knew he'd gotten to the memory of my mother when his face crumpled.

This time it was me who drew him into an embrace, making silly soothing sounds and patting his back awkwardly.

"Is she really gone?" His voice sounded hollow.

"Yes."

"It all feels unreal. As if I wasn't really there."

"You weren't really there. They stole your mind."

"If I could just. If I could..." He shook his head. He couldn't form the sentences.

We stood there for long minutes – too long. Time was too precious, even for this.

"We have to go," I said gently. "I have an army waiting for me to fight the Fae ... and the humans."

His brow wrinkled at that. I'd still need to explain a lot of things.

"And I have someone who I need to save," I said, clearing my throat.

"We need to leave this place, Allie," my father said. "I can't protect you here."

I hesitated. But he was in his right mind now and it was wrong to leave him defenseless. I removed my quiver and bow with care. I'd lost arrows when he plunged me in the water. There were barely a half-dozen left.

"Arrows fired from this bow pierce only evil hearts," I said, handing it to him.

He shook his head. "It's yours, daughter."

"I have the sword," I said, nodding to it. Which was silly because we both knew I didn't know how to use the sword, but my strength didn't lie in my fighting ability. My strength lay in my role and in the army I had recruited. It lay in my cleverness with bargains and my allies.

I pushed the quiver toward him again and he took it this time, slinging it over his shoulder.

"Now what, Allie? I'll admit, my memory is spotty. I am trying very hard, but the pieces are coming back slowly. I can remember losing your mother – stars above, why did she leave like that? I think I should know why, but that hasn't come back." He swallowed awkwardly.

"I need to save my husband," I said firmly. "Tonight."

"Husband? You're far too young for that," my father growled. "I'll skin the man who married you without my permission!"

"Nevertheless," I said, looking away awkwardly. "Will you help me?"

"What choice do I have?"

"None if you want to stay with me," I said with a hard voice. I would not debate this. My heart felt like it had been seared by a hot poker every time I thought of Scouvrel in the merciless hands of the Kinslayer. "And then we go back to the human world and save Skundton and the mortals there and ... well, everything."

His smile was wryly affectionate. "It's a plan."

"And hopefully you'll get your memory back and then maybe you'll know how we can do that. Mom seemed to think the answer was lurking somewhere in your memories."

This time when he nodded, he looked very serious. Those memories must feel as fleeting to him as my plan did to me. I had no idea how to find this Spectacle. And it was happening tonight.

I'd have to risk using the sword. Because there was no way I could find my way there in time if I tried walking across the Faewald. I didn't even know where 'there' was. I didn't know how to use those Nightshades to get there and I had no wings or mount to carry me. My only hope was a gamble. I'd slash into the mortal world and then slash back here and hope beyond hope that it would be quick enough and that I would not lose too much time.

"Perhaps you should see to your army first and your husband after?" my father said, and I realized I had already drawn the sword and I was staring at it for far too long.

I probably should. If I left now and rounded up my army, I could stop Anabetha and Hulanna before they waged war again. That should be my primary responsibility.

And yet ...

I couldn't leave Scouvrel to his fate. When I'd needed him, he'd done whatever he had to do to be there for me.

I swallowed and swung the sword.

"Husbands first, armies later."

Later in the Faewald ...

"The Conqueror flew through the Faewald ~~like the ray of the sun, roving across the land.~~ She bowed Malentric before her, trapping her and stealing her will. She cowed the very flowers. ~~She stilled the Wild Hunt.~~ She pitted herself against the Spring of Tears, fought against ~~a thousand adversaries~~ and her own father. She rose up and saved us all.

She was the Hunter and like a hawk, diving from the sky, she hunted for righteousness.

The Knave waited, not willing to break the spell before she arrived for his glorious plan had not yet been realized and he was loathe to hinder it in any way. Not even if he had to pass the worst test imaginable ... the test of patience. But he was the most patient of them all, the most glorious, the most beautiful of all the Faewald."

- Tales of the Faewald

Chapter Eight

The sword slashed through the air and cut. I looked back at my father, trying to convey all the determination and hope I needed to feel. His grim smile was enough. With a brisk nod of my head, I pulled my blindfold half up – I wanted to see humans and Fae alike since I didn't know where we'd come out. I fought through my usual dizziness as I stepped through the slash in the air...

...and into chaos.

I came out on a muddy slash of land, churned by so many feet that I couldn't tell if it had once been a creek bed, or grass, or even forest. Arrows littered the ground, some stuck in, some half-swallowed by the mud. Saplings were snapped off and broken into shards. And between the arrows and wreckage, other things jutted up from the mud – things I didn't dare look at too hard. Not with the smell of death and offal rising around us. I gagged, but I had to step forward again to make room for my father.

A roar broke out and I twisted to find it in the twilight. On one side of me, a line of men stood holding torches. Their faces were dirty and bloody. Some held weapons. Some held broken remains of what had once been weapons. Behind them, someone was singing – a terrible, doleful tune sung offkey. They were packed tightly together, breathing too hard, the looks on their faces were close to panic – fear mixed with determination, mixed with surprise at the sight of me. Their weapons, held in trembling hands – were already stained dark.

In a blink, I realized why their eyes filled with terror at the sight of me. Nothing would look so Fae right now as I did – stepping from the slash in the air in bright Fae clothing, spattered in my mother's blood, with an axe handle held above my head in one hand and a sword in the other.

Someone started to scream something, but I knew I didn't dare pause. Not even for this. I slashed the air again. Turning to see if my father was following me.

As I turned, I saw the other side of the slash – saw the line of Fae rippling like a current rushing toward us – their hair streaking behind them as they charged – silently – from what had once been my town. They rode on creatures – pangolins, horses, unicorns, and stags, or ran on their own feet, weapons high, foxy faces violent and hungry with their glamor dropped in the heat of battle. The silence was unnerving. Not a war-cry filled a throat, or a gasp of fear. Their faces were stone. Unrelenting. Unmoved.

My father's eyes widened in horror.

"Come on, Dad!" I yelled. I pulled back the rip in the air and he leapt.

No time. Not for this. Not for anything else.

I hoped with all my heart that I wouldn't be too late – that Scouvrel would not yet be dead. That he would be on the other side of this slash of air.

I opened my eyes as I leapt through the open slash at the same time that the first arrow buried into the mud beside me with a soft *twang*.

I was falling, falling, falling, legs trying to run but only swinging uselessly in the air and then I hit the mossy ground with a smack. My legs hurt. My rear hurt. My body was shaking. But the moss had taken the worst of it.

Beside me, a groan told me my father had landed, too.

"I'm not fond of all this travel, daughter," he moaned.

"Shh!"

But there was no need to *shhh* him over the roar of the crowd around us. This must be the Spectacle.

It had to be.

I didn't want to look – and yet I didn't dare hesitate. I leapt to my feet, thrusting the sword into my belt and swishing my axe handle through the air. If ever I needed invisibility it was now. I grabbed my father's hand in my free hand, whispering urgently.

"Be as quiet as you can. As long as I am holding you, you should be invisible. We are here for my husband and then we run, understand? We're not here for anything else. No matter what else we see."

He nodded, looking wary. The bow was in his other hand, the arrow already nocked, though the string was not yet drawn back.

"I'll admit, Allie," he whispered. "I am not at home here. I can manage the terror – almost – but this place ... I can't be here for long. Or I'll go mad again."

I swallowed, nodding, and yanked my blindfold down. I understood what he meant. When I looked at the Tangled reality of the Faewald, it turned my stomach, too.

But there were worse things than fear and nausea.

Please don't let him be badly hurt, please!

I searched around us for clues. It was night. And that was good because it meant we might be there on the first night of the Spectacle, as I had hoped – perhaps the only night. I didn't know how these things worked.

We were on the back edge of a crowd of Fae who pressed against one another, hopping up and down as they tried to get a better look. There were brownies and grundels, hobgoblins and banshees, fauns, and pixies, and above them, everyone who had wings was hovering overhead. Will-o-the-wisps in floating in groups of a dozen of the same color were trapped in bubble-cages that filled the night sky to illuminate the scene below. Centaurs stomped irritably at the back of the crowd.

I forced my way through the back ranks of Fae. I could see nothing from here. And I needed to see.

The jeers and laughter were making me nervous. They combined with cheers and shouts in a way that made my skin crawl and the faces around me worried me most of all. They were lit with a smug satisfaction and fey excitement that seemed at odds with malevolence and violence that clouded around us. I smelled something in the air – something not unlike the musk of a beaver or skunk – something that suggested territorial claims and deadly defense.

I swallowed uncomfortably, and I felt my father's hand tighten on my own as we forced our way through the throng of Fae. One glance back at the rictus his face was set in reminded me that the fancy clothing, expensive jewels, and magical wonders around us were unseen to him. All he saw was the tangled mess of this place – the bitter evil and horrific hell that the Faewald really was under its glamor. I needed to get him out of here again quickly.

Around us, the Fae cursed and shoved, but they seemed unconcerned by our invisibility. Perhaps the axe handle somehow had the effect of making us not just invisible to their eyes but also to their minds.

When we finally broke out from the crowd to where we could see the platform, it was all I could do not to cling to my father in horror. I gripped his palm tighter and he held mine just as tightly – both of us afraid of losing the other.

Horror shuddered through me at what I saw.

The Kinslayer – it seemed – had truly made a grisly spectacle for the Faewald. He stood on a painted box on top of a wooden platform. A sharp black jacket and form-fitting trousers were his only decoration other than strings of tiny bones that looped around his neck like layered necklaces. He must be wearing twenty or thirty of those. He held a long ring-master's whip in one hand and a smug smile on his powder-blue face told me he was enjoying this.

A frame had been built behind the platform that looked like the gilded edge of an expensive portrait frame. But the people carved into the frame were twisted in horrifying ways, their faces depicted as agonized. Even a glance at it from the corner of my eye made me want to shudder. The area behind the frame was draped with bright red and blue cloth – the perfect background for their Spectacle. It was as if the Travelers had taken one of their dramatic plays and then reimagined it as how hell would conduct that play – and voila. This.

Could I sneak in from behind the curtains? Would anyone be watching from behind that cloth?

I'd tried not to look at the center of the stage until I had evaluated everything else. I needed to be focused. I needed to lead with my head and not my heart.

I took a breath for courage and looked. Big mistake.

A wheel turned in the center of the stage. It had been painted in stripes like the pieces of a pie – red and white stripes alternated around the wheel. A golden band wreathed the edges. picked out with arcane symbols. Affixed to the wheel with iron nails – spiked like one of the living butterflies we'd found in the Balance's home – was my gorgeous Fae husband.

Around him – and in him – were a scattering of throwing knives. Some stuck in the wood. Some in his arms. One was in one of his thighs and another in his belly. One lay next to his neck – as if it had barely missed his throat. A tiny scarlet ribbon edged his neck where the blade had skimmed his throat. Under the knives, long scarlet tears in his chest and wrapping around his back still bled from where the Kinslayer's cat-o-nine-tails had torn him apart when Scouvrel fought for me. Flesh hung raggedly from the tears, torn and dirty.

As Scouvrel spun slowly, around and around so that his head was upright and then his feet were and then his head once more, he smiled almost beatifically – like a suffering angel.

It was so like my Fae husband to take even this with calm. Perhaps he was pleased that at least his suffering was on display. He was not the kind who enjoyed suffering in silence. He would want someone to know and appreciate his every agony.

I swallowed.

I needed to free him. But pulling those spikes out would be no easy task. My hands were slick with sweat at the thought and my mouth was dry as sawdust. How could I get him free with everyone watching? Would he even survive being taken from that wheel?

I felt a tremor start in my hands I'd been right to worry about letting my emotions take over. They were already starting to cripple me. I clenched my jaw and tried to shove them aside.

As I watched, a woman clad in a dress made of red and gold ribbons and nothing else – what was with the Fae and their inability to wear decent clothing? – donned a blindfold and turned her back to Scouvrel. The Kinslayer cracked his whip. She spun and threw the dagger.

My breath caught. Scouvrel didn't even flinch.

The knife bounced off the wheel and fell harmlessly to the stage.

"Which one is your *husband*?" my father whispered in my ear. I could tell it cost him to ask. This probably brought back too many memories.

"The one on the wheel," I whispered back.

But not for long. There *would* be a way to free him. And then I would rain down judgment on these Fae for what they had done.

"A Fae?" Horror was thick in his tone. "You have quite a knack for finding trouble, daughter of mine."

"Just focus on how to get him free."

We angled our way through the crowd, stifled by the inability to communicate. Twice, I bumped into the back of a cheering Fae. I wasn't watching my steps closely enough. My gaze could not break away from Scouvrel. He hissed as the whip cracked open the skin of his torso, splitting one of the thorns magically tattooed there in my honor.

"The game of chance was delightful, Knave," the Kinslayer said, his orange eyes alight. "But there are more games to play while you still live. We should not spend all your life in this single one, don't you think?"

"Are you asking for *my* opinion, Kinslayer?" Scouvrel's voice surprised me. He sounded bored, as if he hadn't even heard the question. I swallowed and my father pushed past me. He tugged me along as I tried to see Scouvrel's face. I lost sight of it as we swept to the side of the stage, angling toward the shadow-wreathed area behind it.

My heart felt like it was being torn as my gaze ripped away from him. In my mind, Scouvrel had been practically indestructible – smarter, faster, more charming than anyone else. He was no one's plaything.

"If you wish to give it," the Kinslayer said generously. "Should we allow him an opinion, friends?"

There was a cheer. If the Fae loved anything, it was violent entertainment. Someone broke out in a dance and the crowd pushed against us as it joined in an elaborate step where one Fae seemed to leap over the head of the next in a wave pattern.

"The crowd agrees!"

"In that case," Scouvrel's voice rang out like a bell. "It is my decided opinion that you are much too dull to host a Spectacle, Kinslayer. A Spectacle should be an art in pain. A long, sumptuous feast on the dismantling of the victim's spirit. It should involve the delight of surprise, the hiss of symmetry, the cry of exhultation as the pieces slide together and the grand theme is revealed. It should utterly ruin every shred of hope, every scrap of humanity, every whisper of decency. In short, it should be creative. But you torture me most with boredom. We've all seen the wheel before. We've all taken turns throwing knives blindly. We've all seen a Fae skewered with iron. It's a shame that Decinda died when she did. A shame that you killed her. She was much more inventive in her role as Kinslayer than you ever were. A real innovator. A trailblazer. Maybe you could try imagining you were her instead of wasting all our time with this child's game."

There was quiet for a moment and in that moment of silence, my father drew me in under the cloth that hung from the back of the stage. Here, the support beams crisscrossed on the back of the stage.

"You married a Fae, Allie of mine?" my father sounded grim.

"It was not by choice ... well, not at first," I protested in a whisper. I was looking for a crowbar – any kind of tool to free Scouvrel with, but of course there were none. This stage was probably built by golems – the iron nails hammered in with their stone fists.

"And now?" he asked.

"And now, I will die trying to free him if that's what it takes," I hissed. And I realized in my bones that it was true. How had that devious Fae gotten so far under my skin that the thought of living without him left me feeling ill? "I know you need an explanation, but can you please be patient? I have a lot going on right now!"

I kissed my father quickly on the cheek. Broke my hand-clasp with him and then scrambled up on the stage. He'd be hidden behind the colored cloth. He was safe until I got back.

The Kinslayer began to laugh. Slowly at first, and then louder and louder, his deep baritone echoing across the crowd until they joined him. It was clearly a laugh for the crowd, not a true emotional response. It sounded forced, even to my mortal ears. Scouvrel had struck a nerve.

I crept across the stage, axe handle held high, inching toward the wheel that stood between me and the crowd.

"I love it when my prey begs," the Kinslayer boomed, the thorns in his skin seeming to pulse as he projected his voice. "I love it even more when their pleas are masked by false bravado. No one believes for a moment that you are so blasé about your fate, Knave. Do we?"

The crowd laughed and cheered, buoyed up by the confidence of their leader. They were all trash. Awful Fae trash. Everything my grandmothers despised.

The most good I could ever do would be wiping their kind off the map.

I slipped around the wheel so that I was standing right next to Scouvrel as the Kinslayer began to speak again. I blocked him out. He was only egging the crowd on as they suggested the next torture.

It was worse being so close to Scouvrel that I could reach out and touch the hot blood trickling from his wounds, that I could see the red blisters around the iron nails through his skin, that I could feel his labored breaths on my skin.

"My husband," I whispered right in my ear.

"My Nightmare," he almost seemed to sag with relief as one corner of his mouth turned upward in half of an evil smirk, though his eyes did not meet mine since I was invisible to him. They gazed out into the middle-distance. "Can you hear her?"

"Hear who?" I whispered as I gripped one of the nails and tried to rip it out.

"Death, my Nightmare. She sings her siren song and calls me to her."

"Then tell her to go sing to someone else," I said. "You are *my* husband, not hers."

"Is there a difference?" he sighed. "Her embrace is the same as yours – cold, hard, and unyielding."

"I see they haven't injured your flattering tongue," I said wryly, but I was worried. I wasn't making any progress at all, and behind me, I heard the Kinslayer crack his whip.

"Let the game begin!" the Kinslayer cried.

"Go, Nightmare," Scouvrel whispered urgently. "I shall die with your name on my lips. My last thoughts shall be of you."

"They will be," I assured him. "But that won't be for a long time."

I turned, shoving the axe handle into my belt.

The crowd gasped as my invisibility faded away. Time to take a gamble.

"I'm here to restore the Balance," I announced.

Chapter Nine

There was a gasp – but it was a delighted one. There is nothing the Fae like so much as drama. And I was giving them that. Even the Kinslayer sucked in a delighted breath before his brow furrowed and his eyes widened.

"You," he gasped. "The daughter."

"I am many things," I said breezily. "Daughter is only one of them."

I did not feel breezy. I felt furious. They had reveled in my husband's pain and planned his death. Now I was going to make them pay for that. It should be easy. They'd already disrupted order, and as the Balance, I could get it back, couldn't I? That was how my magic worked.

"You are the one who broke into my home and released my butterflies," the Kinslayer said.

"Next time you should pin up something your own size."

"I did," he said showing all his teeth as he pointed at Scourvel. "Shall we find another wheel for you? I'm not giving up my games. Not even for the daughter of the mortal I lured to spend an entire day here. Not even for the girl who is likely my own blood."

"I'm Hunter's daughter, not yours," I said calmly. If my mother said that, then it was true. I reached for Balance, but there was no magic when I reached for it. There was nothing at all. I swallowed, feeling suddenly empty. What had happened to me? Under my feet, I felt the wooden platform shift and when I looked down, flowering vines were sprouting from the wood around my feet.

Fat lot of good they did. I needed magic, not garnishes.

"Is that what she told you? Is that the lie she gave?" his voice was low. There was a hushed excitement in the crowd as their eyes followed us back and forth.

"It's the truth," I said grimly. "And now, I demand a tax."

That had to be right. The last Balance taxed them for everything.

The Kinslayer froze, tilting his head. "What kind of tax?"

"A pain tax. For every four wounds my husband suffered, you will suffer one the same."

"Husband?" the Kinslayer laughed. "Your marriage is complete?"

I looked back at Scouvrel just in time to see one of the nails fall from his hand. I spoke quickly and loudly to disguise the sound of it hitting the stage.

"We are married."

The Kinslayer's laugh was wicked. "Then you can't collect tax for him, Balance. Can't you feel that you are unable to reach your power? He is left vulnerable by your false assumptions. You could slay us on the behalf of any Fae we wronged – any of them except him. Because it isn't justice if you do it on behalf of your lover. That's revenge."

I heard a plink sound from behind me. I needed to keep their attention on me.

"If revenge is what it's called, then I guess that's what I'll be getting," I said, drawing my rusty sword. I needed to look dramatic. I needed all eyes on me. There was a moan from behind me, so I raised the sword high and proclaimed. "Who will fight me for his life?"

"With a rusty sword?" the Kinslayer scoffed. "I'd hoped for better from my kin. But if this is all you have, then I'll be delighted to kill you."

His whip cracked above my head at the same moment that I heard Scouvrel fall to the ground behind me.

The Kinslayer's face went white at the same time that a dagger spun through the air toward him from behind me. I didn't wait to see who had thrown it. I slashed the air with the sword, ripping a path to the human world.

I looked behind me in time to see Scouvrel swaying, pale, blood pouring from half a dozen wounds as he clutched his belly. He couldn't stand like that. He certainly couldn't flee.

My father stepped out from behind the wheel and lifted Scouvrel in a single motion, his face grim and deadly.

I pulled back the side of the rip at the same time that the Kinslayer whipped again, catching my sword with the tip of his whip. I pulled against his whip, refusing to lose my magical sword, but he was too powerful.

The sword ripped from my hands, tumbling out into the crowd as my father pushed past me, leaping into the rip with Scouvrel in his arms. I looked out at the sea of wicked faces and swallowed. There was no way to get the sword back. I'd lost it. And with it, I'd lost a huge advantage.

Biting back a curse, I leapt after them, through the rip in the world.

At least we had Scouvrel back – for as long as he survived.

Chapter Ten

We plunged into the mortal realm into the dark and the pouring rain. I tugged my blindfold up to try to see but immediately pulled it half down again. I needed to be able to see Scouvrel and it was too dark to see anything else. My father set him down on the ground where he curled around his belly, huffing and moaning. He was mortally injured. Of that, I was sure.

"Now we talk. Right now. You married this Fae?" My father sucked in an angry breath. The night was so dark that I couldn't see his face. "You're only sixteen!"

"Seventeen by now, and not even really that," I said absently. "You and I lost ten years in the Faewald and who knows how much time since. You're in your late forties now, even if you look like you're in your late thirties."

But though I was talking to him, I wasn't looking at him. My eyes scanned Scouvrel, looking for any other injuries I might have missed.

"And Genda? Your sister? Are all my memories true?"

"I guess it depends on what you remember," I said as I ran my hands over Scouvrel. He flinched from the wounds in his shoulders and I gently peeled his coat back. The wounds there were bleeding freely with hints of white bone peeking through. I fought against a wave of nausea and tried to look at his belly wound. He shook his head, clamping his hand to it tighter.

"Get me back to the Faewald, Nightmare. I need to heal, and your realm is terrible for that. Terrible."

"I've lost my sword, husband of mine," I said tightly. "And without it, I'm as stuck here as any other mortal."

My own belly felt tight as a bowstring. My head was buzzing with too many thoughts. I didn't want him to die. I hadn't thought this would happen. Not really. I knew he was being threatened but the emotional experience of facing him actually being gone – it had been like a bad story. Something that couldn't possibly be true in the end.

Die. I could barely think the word because every time I did, I saw my mother running through that door again.

My head hurt. My mouth was dry. I was going to pass out.

Stop it, Allie. This is not about you. It's about Scouvrel. Focus on healing him.

"I remember being insane. I remember things your sister did to me – unspeakable things," my father's voice as haunted. "I remember things your mother said. And then she left us through that door." He coughed and it sounded like he was trying to disguise emotion. "We could take your husband to the stone circle."

He was trying to mollify me.

"Not in this rain we can't," I said, blinking water out of my eyes. "I have no idea where we are and in this dark, we'll hurt him tripping over roots and trees. And that's if we don't get lost or walk right into our enemies."

"What did you think of when you swiped the sword. Little Nightmare?" Scouvrel asked tightly.

"I was only thinking of fleeing," I said.

He was going to die like this. He didn't have the strength to fight these wounds without help and everything I had was soaking wet and there was no shelter, no way to start a fire in the middle of this downpour.

"More specific," he gasped.

"I …" I tried to think. "I think I was remembering a deer we spooked when we came out of Fisher's cottage. The way his tail flicked up like a white flag. I wanted to be gone in a second like the deer."

"Cottage," Scouvrel gasped.

"What's he talking about?" my father asked.

"The sword usually took me close to whatever I was trying to get to. I think he hopes we're near that cottage."

But I wasn't hopeful. My thoughts had been scattered and useless. And in this dark, we could be mere paces away and not know it.

"Wait," I gasped. "I forgot."

I still had the axe handle in my hand. In the shock of our return, I'd completely forgotten it. I swiped it in the air. Not far from us, I could see the bank of the river and tucked in neatly beside it was Fisher's summer cabin. It was small and the roof was more moss than anything else, but it should keep the rain off.

"Can you lift him again?" I asked my father.

"Yes, but I can't walk in this. I can't see a thing. I can't even see him."

"I'll guide you," I said. "I can see with my spirit vision and this torch will light my way."

"I thought it made you invisible," my father said as I guided his hands and he lifted Scouvrel again. My husband groaned and I tried not to flinch though he wouldn't see it anyway. His eyes were shut against the pain.

"It does both. Here. I'll guide you."

I moved beside him, gripping his upper arm so I could guide him over the little hillocks and fallen branches to reach Fisher's cottage.

We paused at the doorstep.

"There are steps here," I said. "Three. And then the threshold."

"While I'm flattered to be carried over the threshold," Scouvrel said weakly, "I'm disinclined to marry two members of the same family."

My father growled angrily.

"Ignore him," I said repressively, opening the door for them. "It's just his nature."

"You chose to marry a man who would joke about marrying *me*?" my father scolded. "You should have better taste than that, Allie. I raised you better than that."

Scouvrel laughed weakly and then moaned. "I've undone all her raising."

I hurried into the cabin, found the lantern and the flint and lit it quickly. Real light filled the room and I tugged my blindfold down, stashing the axe handle back into my belt.

I closed the door hurriedly. "Set him on the bed."

My father complied, shaking his head roughly as he hurried to light a fire in the broken circle of rocks in the center of the cabin. Fisher had the fire set up the old way – a broken rock circle with a chimney suspended above it rather than built into a fireplace in one wall the way most people made them now.

"And you, my husband, will not die tonight," I ordered, leaning over the bed to try to remove his sodden jacket. It was useless now – ragged and bloody. I cut it off his body carefully. "Do you hear me?"

"Your mother, Nightmare," he said, his eyes opening just enough that I could see them glittering in his fever-drawn face. "She walked through the Dread Door?"

"Yes," I said. "She used my key."

"No pain? No blood? Just walking through the doors?"

"She was already wounded," I said miserably. "Shot by an arrow."

He grunted and closed his eyes, clearly unhappy. Well. At least he wasn't pleased with my mother's death. I couldn't exactly expect sympathy from him, so I should take what I could get.

I slipped off my pack and rummaged through it. There wasn't much there anymore. But the blanket was still dry. I began to cut it into strips. At the very least, Scouvrel would need bandages.

His head lolled to the side as he faded out of consciousness.

"A Fae, Allie. A heaven-forsaken fae!" my father spat from beside the fire he was kindling.

"You've noticed," I said dryly.

"Don't take that tone with me. I know that sarcastic tongue of yours and you can't hurt me with it."

"I'm not trying to hurt you," I said with a sigh. "I'm glad to see you after all this time."

"To me, it feels like weeks at most – weeks since I had a happy family of four tucked away in our little house."

"It's gone now. The village burnt it to the ground and is using our land as pastureland."

He sucked in a breath and I laid the bandages out carefully beside Scouvrel and stood to search the cabin for a dish of some kind. There was a battered tin bowl that fisher clearly used as a washbasin. I filled it with water from a bucket beside the door and returned to the bed.

"Your mother ..." My father choked on the words.

"She loved you very much," I said gently. I sighed. "As I do. But to be frank, I was thrust out into the world of taking care of other people quite suddenly and I had to manage as I could."

"Your mother wouldn't want you married to ... one of them. Fair Folk. She hated them."

"With good reason, it would seem." I couldn't keep the bite from my words. "I wonder why she didn't tell us that she'd been there. That she'd known them."

"People make mistakes."

I looked up. "You don't sound surprised."

He raised an eyebrow.

"You knew," I said, stunned. "Did that make it easier or harder when Hulanna disappeared?"

"Harder." His voice was grim.

"But you still tried to save her," I said softly. I wet a rag and began to dab the wounds at Scouvrel's shoulders. They were burned around the edges from the iron, the skin bubbling up like a boiling pot frozen in mid-bubble. I tried to be gentle, but Scouvrel moaned in his sleep. I flinched at the sound. I hated causing him pain. It seemed as if I could feel it, too.

"I tried to save her from herself. Just like I'll try to save you. Listen to me, Allie."

I spared a glance for his earnest expression before returning to my work, wrapping one shoulder with a clean bandage. The gashes needed stitches. But first, they'd need to be cleaned.

"This marriage – it's not a mortal marriage. You can walk away and live a normal life. Whatever you've been tricked into – whatever you've vowed. It doesn't matter now. You can leave him here once you've dressed his wounds. He'll be safe enough, so that won't be on your conscience. And then you and I will hike out of here. I was north of here once – a long time ago, I was barely older than you. I hiked through the mountain pass and into the Kingdom of Couvresal. It's a nice place. Cold. Poor. But nice enough. I didn't stay, but you and I could. We can leave all this behind and go make a new life. And I'll protect you. I'll take care of you. I'll help you find a nice human man to marry, if that's what you want – a good man. A faithful man. The kind of man you deserve. Hmmm?"

I could see myself in that world. I could see myself hunting with my father again, a big smile on his face when we sighted game, and an even bigger one when we took it down. I could imagine a cottage like this one somewhere in this mountain kingdom he remembered. I wouldn't mind being poor. And I could see a hazy face in my mind that kept changing – a male face and then perhaps little children's faces.

I could be happy like that. I could live that life.

But wouldn't I always wonder if one day I would see a flash of a wing or the horn of a unicorn, or a girl dancing around a circle? Wouldn't I wonder if my sister was just over the horizon, about to lead an army to conquer my new land and laugh as we died beside our loved ones? Wouldn't I worry every time one of my children was out of my sight that he or she had been snatched by Fae hands and dragged off to the living nightmare of the Faewald?

I would never find peace again.

It wasn't even an option.

Besides, it was unlikely I could ever live with someone else like I'd been living with Scouvrel.

I wasn't even sure that I wanted to. It would be wrong to feel this strongly about anyone else.

I swallowed as I worked to clean and dress his other shoulder. His eyes were closed, his long black lashes fanning out over his cheeks in such an innocent way that it almost seemed sacrilegious on someone so wicked. Across his jaw a light stubble had grown, marring the perfect lines of his jaw and cheekbones. He was unconscious now. Maybe even dreaming. And if he had nightmares, then I knew they were of me.

Across his arms and chest were my marks – my thorns for my prickly nature – and slicing through them and all around them were the many scars he'd borne for me – including these new, horrific injuries. I hadn't even looked at the belly wound yet – I was almost too afraid to look. Almost too terrified to imagine how bad it might be.

I pulled thread from my pack and readied it to start stitching the tears where the Kinslayer's whip had flayed him.

He might die tonight in this little cottage. And if he did, then with him would die the only Fae to ever dream of redeeming their awful lot. The only one who ever made my heart sing and my belly laugh. The thought of that left me feeling so hollow – so unmoored that I shied away from it completely.

I didn't dare admit it – not even to my father – but I didn't think I wanted to live in a world where he was not. I didn't want to live that happy life in the mountains without a single jab or taunt from these twisting lips, without the caress of his deceptive charm or the heady excitement of trying to bargain with him for basic things.

I hadn't meant to do this.

I hadn't meant to fall in love.

I swallowed and prepared another cloth, gently pulling his hand away from his belly so I could look at the damage.

"Allie?" my father pressed.

I blinked hard. Was I crying? Ridiculous.

I shook my head and sniffed, clearing my tears. Enough of this. I'd just have to try to save his life and if I failed, I would mourn him with my mother ... later.

"No," I said, as I tried to sop up enough blood to properly see Scouvrel's wound. It was bleeding so hard that it kept filling again. I swallowed. This was really bad. I didn't know how to fix it. "I'm not leaving him and I'm not ending my marriage. I chose this, Dad. And if you don't like it, well that's just too bad."

"Allie." He sounded horrified.

"Listen, Dad," I said, making my face as hard as I could. "I love you and I'm glad to have you back to your right mind. And I'm really sad about Mom and I don't know what to say about that. But I've made my choice and I'm not leaving Scouvrel. And if you don't like that ... well, you don't have to stay here. Go to Couvresal. Go wherever you want."

My eyes stung but I refused to cry. I didn't know what I was doing, but at least I knew that would be a bad idea.

"Why?" he pressed. "Why do you cling to him? You don't owe him anything."

"Because I love him," I said sharply. "Can you understand that?"

I checked Scouvrel's face. He hadn't heard me, had he? It remained slack – thank goodness.

My father let out a long breath. "What kind of ridiculous name is Scouvrel, anyway? No real man would put up with a name like that."

But he didn't object anymore. Instead, he filled a kettle beside the fire. After a while, he spoke while I pushed a piece of blanket hard against Scouvrel's belly wound. It needed stitching. But I was just as worried about doing that and locking something in there as I was about not doing it and letting him bleed too much.

"I can make a basic poultice, but don't expect much."

"Thank you," I said, feeling my eyes growing puffy again at his kindness. I felt like I might start crying at any moment. Which was utterly ridiculous.

"And tomorrow we'll bring him to the stone circle ... if he lives that long. He seemed to think he could survive better in his world."

I began to thread the needle I'd pulled from the pack. Fortunately, it was brass and not steel. Better stop the bleeding, I supposed. Even if it meant closing a wound that might not be repaired inside. And then I'd mend those nasty tears.

"You should think about whether you can survive it," my father said gently. "Sometimes you can love things that are wrong. If you're wise, you'll find a way to walk away from them. Otherwise, they'll kill you."

He was right, of course. But I wasn't even sure if I cared about that anymore.

Chapter Eleven

It was a tough night.

I spent it awake beside Scouvrel after I stitched up what wounds I could, almost jumping every time he moaned or gasped. There was little I could do for him. I applied the hot poultice my father had made. I kept pressure on his wound until the bleeding eased – but he was feverish and sweating and I knew this wasn't good.

I'd never seen him like that before – so vulnerable and weak. So very mortal looking. Could he die like this? Probably not in the Faewald, but I didn't think the rules were the same in the mortal world and that worried me.

The rain beat down on the roof for what felt more like weeks than mere hours and as I wiped Scouvrel's brow and whispered to him, my anxiety only increased. How could we even get him back to the Faewald like this? And if we did, wouldn't we be immediately vulnerable? We couldn't just go exactly where we wanted to. We would pop out next to the Smoke Waterfall and there wasn't anywhere close to take cover.

On top of that, I had to get a hold of my army. I'd seen the Fae and the humans lining up to fight during our hop through the Faewald. That could have been hours ago or weeks ago – and either way, it wasn't good. That battle had been ugly – intense – devastating. And where *was* my army? I hadn't seen them there.

On the other side of the room, in the only other cot, my father slept. His sleep was fitful, and he thrashed in his blankets as often as he broke into a rattling snore. Every time he sighed my mother's name, I fought back tears. Sitting here – on a stool between Scouvrel's cot right next to me and my father's on the other side of the room – I felt was fitting. I was caught between the two – my life as a mortal Hunter and my life as the Balance and the wife of Scouvrel. What did that mean for me? Where did I owe my loyalty and sacrifice?

Eventually, I pulled out the book Scouvrel had left me and flipped through the pages. A note fluttered out of it.

It read:

My Nightmare, Haunter of my Dreams, Ghoul of my Darkest Hours,

I dream of a life with you in a time beyond this one where you may torment me day after day in whatever fashion suits you best. I am certain you will find yourself to be very creative.

If this note has found its way to you it means I am either dead or certain I will be shortly. I beg you not to mourn me and I release you of the burden of avenging me. If you return to my home in the Eye of the Knave where I left my painting for you, you will find two things that may warm your heart.

The first is my missing ear, dried and preserved for your enjoyment. I procured it back from those who first bought it from me – at a much lower cost, so they clearly are unfit to bargain.

The second is a large onyx ring which I hope will remind you of my black eyes even as it has reminded me of your black heart.

Cherish these things and the certain knowledge that my love for you rivals even the deep-rooted wickedness in the depths of my heart.

Your husband,
The Knave

How incredibly like Scouvrel to mix sweet words with insults and hints of evil. I glanced over at him and saw his eyes slit open. He hissed but he managed a slight wicked curve of a half-smile.

"Nightmare. I must still be dreaming because you are still here."

"Finmark," I breathed, enjoying his slight shudder at the sound of his name. I couldn't help it. I loved saying it. I loved how it made him nervous and happy all at once.

He pushed himself up from the bed, but I leaned over and tried to push him back down. "Don't get up. You're going to hurt yourself."

He glanced over at my father and I wondered why he would do that until he grabbed my wrists and pulled me to him with surprising strength.

"I'm not dead yet, wife," he whispered, and then his lips caught mine, his teeth snagging on my lower lip and biting lightly before he moved his hands from my wrists to the sides of my face, cradling it as he kissed me. There was a violence to it – as if he was fighting the pain as he kissed me as if he was denying death her due just to wrap me in a last embrace. I did not fight it. I kissed him back with equal passion. If I was to be a widow soon, I would not mind a moment of being a wife.

The taste of him was a heady thing. It filled my senses as the soft caresses of his lips against mine left me gasping and shuddering. I savored every sensation, letting them burn into my memory. Each taste of him leaving me wanting just one more.

He gasped as he broke away and his breath – shockingly sweet when it should have been disgusting after a night lying here wounded – gusted across my neck in a way that felt too intimate. I glanced over my shoulder at my sleeping father.

"I don't like him," Scouvrel growled. "He thinks he owns you."

"He's my father," I said drily.

"He's not your keeper." He pulled me down with his hands on either side of my face so that he could kiss my ear – the ear, I realized, that matched his missing one. What was with the Fae and ears anyway?

"Neither are you."

"Hmmm." His growl sounded like he might object to that. "You said that your mother sacrificed herself."

His kisses moved to my neck.

"Is that how you interpret that?" I asked, trying to keep my tone to a whisper to keep from waking my father, but trying not to let it turn sultry. This was bad enough in a tiny cabin with my father there! I could feel my cheeks burning already.

"Where is your sister?"

"I don't know. She got free somehow when my mother ran through the doors."

"I'll admit … I had a tiny hope. A hope that is now extinguished." His fingers tangled deliciously in my hair as he moved my face to where he could look into my eyes. Always, looking into his eyes filled me with mixed emotions. There was so much there – trickery and deception, constant calculations, and these days something that looked almost like devotion.

For no reason at all, my heart rate sped up.

"What hope did you have?" I asked in a tiny voice.

"The story of the Substitute made me almost think that it could be done again, that perhaps if a mother loved her child enough ..." He shook his head as his words trailed off.

I shook my head, sadly. I wouldn't have wanted that anyway. My mother shouldn't have died at all. Not to spare me and not for any other reason.

"We have to be responsible for our own lives," I said. "We can't let someone else take that on."

His laugh was mocking. "This from you, Little Hunter? This from you who feels she is responsible to take the place of all mortals everywhere in fighting their fate? This from you who would raise her own army to that end?"

"Someone has to," I said defensively. "I should be there already, leading them to end this. I should never have left them."

"But you did," he whispered. "Because you knew." Here he kissed my forehead, the gesture surprisingly sweet. "Because you knew it's always been about more than you. More than me. More than mere mortal lives that are nothing but a flash of light and then the endless darkness."

"You can't mean that." I breathed. "Not when you kiss me like this."

He pulled my face to his and kissed me again – more desperately than ever, his lips crushing mine with their intensity. I thought I might be tasting blood where his teeth had caught the edge of my lips. It felt – ridiculously right – to be so intertwined, so close that I could feel his flinch and gasp when the pain of his wounds finally overcame him. Rather than drawing back, that only seemed to fuel the fire of his passion.

"I swear, your taste is far finer than your looks, Nightmare. Like fine wine in a flawed bottle."

"How flattering." And yet, I couldn't help the fluttering low in my belly at his words. I leaned in to kiss him again and the fluttering only intensified.

"Did you mean what you said to that old mortal?" he asked.

"My father?" I barely suppressed a chuckle at his frown.

"You told him you loved me."

"I –" I began, but before I could speak, he'd pulled me in for another hungry kiss. It made my mind feel hazy, like I couldn't hold on to a proper thought. I gasped for air, almost not wanting to breathe if it meant I could have more kisses.

"I'm still here," my father's voice broke wryly through our desperate kisses and I pulled back, aghast.

Scouvrel snickered wickedly. "Oh, we knew that, mortal."

I thought my face might burst into flames. I pressed my lips together, biting them inside my mouth.

Scouvrel only laughed more but his laughter turned immediately to a moan and his hands clutched his belly. I gasped as I realized that blood had soaked through his bandages and into a wide red stain around him on the cot.

"Truth or lie, Scouvrel," I asked in a wavering voice. "You're dying."

"Truth, Nightmare," he said with a bitter smile. His eyelids fluttered as if he was fighting for consciousness. "My only regret is that I did not steal that whip from the Kinslayer. I could have done lovely things with that. But I shall treasure the memory of your goodbye as my life slips away. It has been the single most cherished of all my moments. May you haunt me forever."

His lids fluttered shut and then his lips parted as he passed out.

Chapter Twelve

"Scouvrel? Scouvrel?" I called but I knew it was a waste of time. The cot as getting wetter as the blood seeped out of him, soaking it. I hadn't realized he was getting worse. I hadn't realized ...

"You truly want this ... Fae ... saved?" my father asked. He was hunched beside the bank of coals that had been the fire, playing with one of the rocks on the edge of it. The other rocks looked almost like they had been mortared in place – so much ash and dirt had sealed the cracks around them that they formed a solid circle except for the one place where the traditional rock had been removed and set by the door as a doorstop instead. My father was holding the doorstop.

"Yes," I said firmly. "No matter how much the two of you hate each other, you're both ..."

"Both what?" he looked tense, like he might spring at any moment. I was going to make him angry if I finished that sentence. Did I dare do that when I'd only just got him back? But I had to say it. For myself, if no one else.

"You're both family to me."

His jaw tensed and a muscled jumped out from the side of his cheek like he was grinding his teeth but after a moment he nodded sharply and placed the doorstop in the stone circle, completing it.

I gasped as the view of the fire vanished and the circle filled instead with waving grass and part of a Fae skeleton-windchime filled it instead. A cold wind blew into the cabin, the white light of the Faewald blowing in with it.

"Impossible."

"Not really," my father said bitterly. "There is a reason we don't make stone circles. In the past, they used to do this from time to time. It only makes sense that it would happen now, too. It's circle time."

"Circle time?" I asked.

"The time when the boundaries are paper thin and the Faewald and our world are very close. I don't want to go back there, Allie. My time there – it is like a nightmare I don't want to remember. I'm a grown man. I shouldn't be terrified of a *place* and yet I am."

"Then you shouldn't have to go back." I rose from the stool and crossed to him, offering him a hug. He patted my back gently but stepped back almost immediately.

"That Fae said something about an army."

"Yes," I said. "I brought my own army here. To send all the Fae back to the Faewald and to clear the human armies out of Skundton."

He nodded and sighed. "Then you need to go and get your army and make that happen, Allie. Our ancestors didn't build this land just to see it from the hereafter and mourn as it is occupied by enemies."

"I thought you wanted to run away. To head through the pass."

"That was when thought I could save you, daughter." He laughed grimly. "Clearly, you have too much of your mother and me in you. You've taken on the cares of the world as if they were your own. And you're too far grown for me to stop you. So. Go find your army and end this."

I looked at Scouvrel lying so pale on the cot as his blood dripped to the floor. I didn't think I could leave him. Not while he was still breathing. Maybe not even after.

My eyes were stinging again. Traitors.

My father cleared his throat. "I'll take this Fae through the circle and if he has some ability to heal himself there – well, let that be as it may."

"You will?" I couldn't help my shock. "I thought you just said it was a nightmare."

"I'll walk another nightmare for you, Allie," my father said, the wrinkles around his eyes creasing as he smiled at me. "I'll take every nightmare if it spares you pain. I'm your father. Just remember, it's for *you* not for ... it."

"Thank you." I spoke slowly as if lingering on the word. I had to go – and yet I couldn't bear to tear myself from the two of them.

"Here," he said, passing the bow and quiver back to me.

I shook my head. "You need them. I still have the sewing needle."

He looked at the needle in my belt curiously as I moved it to the scabbard, but he didn't say anything about it. "I won't be able to use it if I'm taking care of him. Just take the bow."

"Then you take my pack. There's a tent, a blanket, a bottle of water, a pot, a flint, and some other things," I said, reaching into the pack and pulling out the book and mirror. I slipped them into my pockets and jammed the book my mother had helped me find into the pack. "Use them to keep yourselves safe while he heals." When I was done, he strapped it on his back before he hefted Scouvrel from the cot. My husband's head lolled in a way that made me swallow down a lump of fear.

"I love you," I said, and I didn't know if I was talking to my father or my husband.

"Stay safe," my father replied and with a quick nod to me, he stepped into the circle and strode out of it into the Faewald.

My hands were cold and tingling as they left. Every single fibre of me wanted to follow. But I couldn't do that. I had work to do here. Carefully, I filled my waterskin, took a drink, and hung it from my belt. I slipped the novel, the magic book and mirror into my pockets. My load was getting lighter and lighter but there was no time to dwell on that.

I had an army to find and a battle to wage. I might never see Scouvrel or my father again. I might not live the day out.

And yet I'd never felt more certain that I was doing the right thing.

BOOK TWO

When the darkness had nearly overwhelmed us, she arose, the hero meant to save us all. ~~Her beauty stunned us, and her great wit rendered us speechless as~~ she strode through the Faewald. She ~~was light and strength~~, a hunter of the mortal world, and a conqueror of the Faewald. And in her path, the Faewald was changed forever, she trampled it under her feet and at her every footstep, blossoms rose, ~~for she was everything good and right and pure~~.

-Tales of the Faewald

Chapter Thirteen

It was still pouring when I left Fisher's cabin. I'd stumbled over the steps before I remembered to pull my blindfold back up.

Come on, Allie, get it together.

The rain soaked through my bloodstained jacket as I strode through the half-light of a rainy dawn. Little rivulets cut through the forest floor and over the path, leaving the way slick and muddy as I tried to move quickly. How many days had it been since the confrontation we'd seen? Were there any people still alive?

I tightened the blindfold, worried I'd miss something. I froze. Wait. I'd only see the Fae with my spirit vision, which meant I'd have to choose the dizzying option of one eye blindfolded and one eye not. With a sigh, I adjusted it, blinking against the double vision.

Interesting. There was a trail of color around the cabin – not going into it, but just around it. A deep charcoal trail that was hard to see but judging by how thick it was, it was fairly fresh. I followed it down the path where two more charcoal paths met up and then all three of them merged and veered off the path.

Curiouser and curiouser.

I stepped off the path to follow, fighting the snatching arms of trees and the wet leaves that slapped my face as I pushed through the dense undergrowth. Everything smelled of rain and dead worms and spruce trees – a mingling of beautiful and disgusting that was almost Fae in its pairing.

I came out in a low dip in the ground – a little wrinkle in the landscape I didn't have a clear memory of. We didn't usually hunt close to Fisher's cabin. That wouldn't have been respectful.

The valley had a strange structure. It was formed by a dip in the ground, but the dip was scattered with huge boulders coated in a thin lichen. Odd. Boulders that size made sense near the mountains, but we were a good hike away from the slopes and the river wouldn't have deposited stones into this round basin, not even if it used to flow here. If it did, they would have followed the flow of a river instead of just being heaped in one place.

I cleared my throat. The rain was giving me the sniffles.

One of the rocks moved.

I froze.

"BALANCE."

I gasped. Could it really be so easy? I'd gone looking for the army and it was right here?

"Hello?" I asked, feeling foolish.

"YOU RETURN."

"Yes," I said, swallowing. "I'm back. Ummm. Do you know where the other golems are? Where Rocky is?"

The stony golems looked around at each other and then one of them started to laugh. I stiffened. This was not good. Was it possible that someone could have turned them? Could have offered them a better deal?

My feet were swept out from under me before I had a chance to gasp. I was dangling from a stone fist, my fingers trailing only inches above the ground before I'd even noticed the golem moving.

"What are you doing?" I asked, but none of them spoke. The only sound was the sound of stones walking through the woods, trampling trees, and clattering across other rocks as they went.

With every footstep, my drenched hair raised more and more on end until a chill set in my bones. If I had lost my army, what would I do now? How could I possibly fight back? And how was I going to get out of this stone grip?

I held onto my things with my hands, trying to keep them all in my pockets, ducking and swinging myself to avoid hitting fallen trees or low-hanging branches as they carried me, swinging, through the forest.

My mind raced furiously. There had to be a way to get them back. Whoever had stolen their loyalties couldn't offer what I was offering ... could they?

My teeth were chattering by the time we began to climb the mountain toward the cave where I'd first discovered that the blindfold could make me see – where I'd first begun to play with magical items – where I'd first ...

I was dumped on the ground with no warning. I cursed, rolling up onto my feet and wringing out my long, rain-soaked braid.

In front of me was Rocky, staring with the impassive face of a stone statue.

"This is a fine way to repay me for my kindness," I said with a scowl.

"WE FIGHT. WE FIGHT, NOW," Rocky said and my eyebrows rose.

Well, that's what you get for trusting people. I drew my needle from the scabbard and settled into what I hoped was a fighting stance. It would be over before it started. There was no way for me to defend myself against a living mountain.

"Are you ready for this? It's a fight that will cost you everything." My words were brave, but my heart was thundering in my chest.

"WAITED FOR YOU. READY."

I nodded my head and lunged forward.

A huge hand scooped me up. I braced myself, ready to fly through the air and smash into the rocks.

Instead, I landed on Rocky's shoulder. He pointed from the peak of the mountain, out across the mountainside that was covered in golems all facing the same way – not toward me, but toward Skundton where a fire blazed, filling the sky with smoke.

"GO!" he ordered, and a hundred stone feet stepped forward with a sound like an earthquake beginning.

Chapter Fourteen

I closed my mouth with a click. I thought they'd turned against me. I thought I had lost them.

Instead, they'd gathered themselves into a force that could move at a single wave from Rocky. He motioned to his golem allies, a quick raise of one arm and then two fingers showing and then a quick gesture to one side of his body.

They fell into two lines easily as if they had been practicing for weeks at this.

"How did you find them all again?" I asked in awe.

"NEW ARMY."

I'd thought giving him a voice would make things easier, but perhaps it was hard for him to speak than I'd bet on. It was the only thing that made sense of his refusal to say more than a few words at a time.

"We can't just run in there. I think they might be fighting."

"LAST NIGHT. WAR."

"Okay, so if they were fighting last night, they might still be fighting. Or someone might have won. Either way, we have a certain goal. We need to round them up and stop the fighting. The humans must be made to go home. The Fae must be made to go back to the Faewald. We aren't here to kill them all – or any of them if we can help it. We're here to make peace."

"DEATH IS PEACE."

"Sure," I agreed, "But that's the wrong kind of peace. We want the kind of peace that lasts."

"DEATH LASTS."

"Have I mentioned that I'm essentially good? That I don't kill for no reason?"

"WE HAVE REASON."

"Could we at least agree that running full tilt in two lines is not the best strategy? It would be better to form a circle around both armies if we can – a loose circle, at least. And then no one can escape or flank us. And then we have the golems all march slowly forward so that we squeeze them together in one space. Then, we'll have their attention and the advantage and that way I can convince them to end this."

"OR KILL."

"Hopefully, it won't come to that."

He paused but then his hand shot up and the army stopped with a lurch. I clung to his forehead, trying to keep from being thrown off his shoulder. Rocky raised both hands and I rocked side to side as I tried to avoid being jarred loose. He spread his fingers.

Immediately, ten other golems left the ranks and spread out before him. He made a motion with his hand like a circle that was slowly narrowing.

"CIRCLE. PEN THEM IN."

"YES," the ten said in unison because that wasn't spooky at all.

"THEN DRAW IN. NONE ESCAPE."

They all nodded. "YES."

I shivered. It *was* spooky. I didn't like it by half.

Rocky was making other motions – specifics, I realized as the groups began to scatter, running out after the first two leaders who swung north and south to start forming the circle. The next two followed as soon as their golems had all left, pounding a trail into the forest.

"NOW WAIT," Rocky said, standing still in a way that only a statue can.

He was right. If our army was going to encircle the town, it was going to take a while. I pulled out the book to read. It was the small glowing book – the one that lit my face blue as I read it. I let the blue light wash over me and tried to find words in the miserly book.

"If the half of the Oolag that is the air is sacrificed, then the doors will be open and any Fae in the mortal world will feel the call to return. Their magic will die in the mortal world. Their powers will weaken. They will be drawn back to the Faewald and though there will be no barrier anymore between sky and sky or land and land, they will not be able to conquer the mortal world, for this is the rending, this is the breaking. This is the time of the circle."

The air half – that was my sister. The one who rends and tears. It wasn't talking about destroying the mortal world. It was talking about opening the doors forever. Maybe that was why the stone circle in Fisher's cottage had opened a path to the Faewald with no additional magic. Maybe the whole world was like my sword had been now – all you had to do was make a stone circle and the barriers between the two worlds melted away.

But my sister hadn't been sacrificed. I hadn't killed her. She'd just disappeared when my mother stepped through that door. Right?

I felt a chill of realization.

Unless Scouvrel was right, and my mother had died in her place – as a substitute. Could that be possible?

It had been possible once before.

But why would she choose my sister instead of me?

I looked back at the book.

"If the half of the Oolag that is the earth is sacrificed, then the doors will be open, and the Fae shall feel the draw to go to the mortal world. Their magic will flourish there. Their powers will abound. They will be drawn to overwhelm the mortal court and there will be no barrier anymore between sky and sky or land and land, so they will conquer the mortal world, for this is the repair, the binding, the lashing. This is the time of the circle."

Did my mother know this? Had she made a choice in whether she had sacrificed herself for Hulanna or for me? And had she chosen Hulanna in one desperate attempt to save the mortal world as much as she could? She'd been babbling about saving her girls. About still loving them. Maybe she'd also chosen to do this for Hulanna out of love. Maybe she really hadn't given up on her.

That was so much like her.

I blinked back a tear and stared at the book, sucking the inside of my cheek.

I hadn't had to make that deal with Scouvrel to absolve him for Hulanna's death. Because now she didn't have to die. But I wasn't off the hook. He still needed me to die if he was going to free his precious Faewald.

"If both halves of the Oolag are sacrificed within one year of one another, then this is the end of circle time forever. The end of two worlds Only one will remain. And evil will sleep until it turns to the good and good will flourish until it overcomes evil."

Great. And all I'd have to do is choose to die while everyone else got to keep on living. How grand.

I swallowed and turned another page, but every other page of the book was blank. Very helpful. A magical book that tells you a riddle and then shuts up like a golem. I tucked it back in my pocket. It was getting so small now that only a sentence at a time could fit on a page. Soon, it might disappear altogether.

Waiting with the golems was hard on the patience. They didn't shift or twitch or scratch or chat. They just stood perfectly still, waiting, as one group after another left until there were only two of us left.

I pulled the other book from my pocket, trying to pass the time. This one was Scouvrel's book. There was one more love letter hidden in the pages.

My Nightmare,

Hopefully, by now I have found time to tell you why you must die for the good of the Faewald. Hopefully, I also explained why your sister must die, also. Please, ensure that you live long enough to see her demise first. I would hate to see you waste that precious blood of yours for no reason.

If you are reading this, then likely I can no longer see my great vision come to pass – but perhaps you can.

I have long loved your vicious tenacity, I have admired your fierce determination, your unbridled ambition. You Nightmare of a creature! You and you alone have haunted me through my nights and days. And I am certain, that you could realize this dream without me ... if you choose to. Why not save the Faewald while you save your precious mortal world? You took on the role of their protector and savior. Why not ours, too? Could we not have the scraps from your table even as you feed the bread to mortals?

I shall leave the decision up to you – as it always has been – and hope in your disgustingly generous heart and ridiculously forgiving soul. They have long been both my balm and torment and will continue to be.

Your husband,

The Knave

P.S. Have I mentioned that your frightful freckled skin is now in all my fantasies? After your sharp mind, it may be your most delightful feature.

My cheeks were hot with embarrassment. Maybe I should read the novel instead. That silly, soppy, love story that Scouvrel loved so much.

I started to read it, tucking the letter back into the pages. Why did he love to read this? The heroine needed to be saved in the first chapter after being almost run over by a loose horse. How had that even happened? She couldn't climb a tree or dodge or something? And then she fainted, and the hero had to press his ear to her breast to see if she was still alive. I was already rolling my eyes. This woman was ridiculous. If there was one thing I'd learned in life, it was that no one was coming to save you. You either figured things out yourself or you died, and that was that.

A nagging feeling in the back of my mind reminded me that wasn't quite true. After all, Scouvrel had rescued me more than a few times. But I'd rescued him, too, and I hadn't done it by fainting and failing to evade farm animals.

I shook my head and jammed the book back into my pocket. I should leave it here. It was only weighing me down. But the mere thought of leaving it behind made me blink back tears. Somewhere out there, Scouvrel was likely dying. And he'd loved this book. I couldn't betray him by leaving it behind. Even if it was beyond silly.

I looked at the first page. There was the title, "Abstinence and Absolution" – a silly title for a silly book. And the name of the author, signed in a flourish. Maverick.

The Maverick?

Could it be possible that before he was the Kinslayer, the horrific creature that hunted and tortured my husband had written soppy love stories about mortals?

That put an entirely different spin on his relationship with my mother. Had he thought – somehow – that he was romancing her? *Had* he romanced her? Like int his book? And why had she never mentioned it?

I shook my head. So many questions. So few chances to get answers.

I tucked the book back into my pocket.

Rocky shifted and I drew my bow and one of my last arrows from my quiver. Here we go. Time to try to stop a war with an army of rocks.

No one ever said my life was boring.

Chapter Fifteen

We were moving now, slowly finding our place in the ring.

"It seems too quiet," I muttered. We could hear sounds ahead of us, but not the sounds of conflict – not a clash of swords or the scream of battle. Smoke still hung over the town but that, too, seemed old. If fires had raged beyond cookfires, they were long gone.

Mist rose through the trees, slowly dissipating in the warmth of the late morning. Now that we were nearing the town, I was getting more nervous.

"I should walk," I told Rocky.

"RIDE," he insisted. "TOO SLOW."

He had a point. I kept my bow ready, fussing with the blindfold. There were too many spirit trails here, tangling one over the other, twisting, doubling back.

We reached a runnel of water and Rocky stepped over it with a single step. I bit my lip when I saw what it was – blood. Just like the last time I'd been so close to the town. Would I ever view this village the same when this was over?

It wasn't much longer before we found the first bodies trampled into the mud. I bit my lip and tried not to look too closely. No one should look like that. No one should be treated like that. They'd been left in the mud like refuse, stacked up waist-high in places, as if they'd died on top of each other. I tried to focus on things that wouldn't hurt as much. A sword stuck into the mud. A torn flag still rippling in the wind. A shining bracelet hanging on a branch. Anything that kept me from seeing the human carnage.

The dead were mostly human, but there were Fae in the glimpses I was seeing, too. Green-skinned orcs with jutting lower jaws and black tattoos, horned Fae lay twisted around their mounts, their strange beauty faded to nothing in death. They looked almost more animal than human once their life was gone. Feral. Strange. Their faerie beasts were just as dead – stuck through with a hundred arrows or hamstrung and then bled out. They littered the muddy fields outside of town like discarded festival booths fallen over after a fierce night of revelry.

I swallowed down bile. I tried to keep my gaze on the town in the distance. What good would it do if I froze in the middle of this? None at all.

There was a roar up ahead and finally, the clash of weapons and the unnerving laughter of the Fae. I should find that frightening. Instead, I found it hopeful. Someone out there remained alive.

We carried on, Rocky's golem footsteps neither wavering nor slowing. If he felt jarred by the death surrounding us, he didn't show it. I was just glad he'd insisted on carrying me, or I would be knee-deep in the dead. I couldn't handle that. Not even to end a war.

I kept my face hard and tense, trying not to betray the fear that coursed through me. The battle really had waged yesterday, and hundreds – maybe even thousands – had died. Whoever still lived was battling on ahead of us. I needed to be ready to face them. A sobbing, vomiting girl wouldn't earn their respect.

I needed to let that Allie burn up in my mental flames so that this Allie could fight.

Come on, Allie. Feed it to the flames. Don't let fear or horror control you.

We could see the nearest golem on each side, but none of the others since we were so spread out, but every step that Rocky took brought us closer and with every one, I was more nervous. What would I say to them when I finally found the Fae? How would I make sure this ended? There had to be a way.

We slipped through the trees and into the cleared area around Skundton.

A gasp ripped from my throat.

The battleground was exactly as I'd seen when I'd burst into the mortal world last night – only hours of battle since then. The muddy space between the edge of the forest and the town was trampled into thick mud and littered with bodies. On one side, a thick band of Fae formed, laughing and joking. On the other, a tight-faced, nervous line of humans faced them.

They were all watching something in the center of the field. With horror – I realized what it was. A duel was taking place in the mud between the two sides. A duel between my sister – when had she learned to fight with a sword? When had she learned to dance and weave like an adder? She was laughing – bright happy peals of laughter – as she dodged and struck, her long hair streaming behind her like a flag.

Her opponent looked far more ragged and rundown. Sir Eckelmeyer's exhaustion lined his face, and there was still a trace of a limp in his movements – a reminder of Scouvrel's branding. But he was holding his own, his huge, double-handed sword was iron and four times the size of my sister's blade. Despite his sword's size, he was quick as a whip.

On either side of the competitors, their armies had raised banners on carved saplings. Each banner had a head decorating the top of the pole. I didn't look at them for long. The very sight turned my stomach. A quick glance told me all I needed to know – the Fae had a head with a fancy helmet stuck on a pole – a Knight I recognized from when I'd been dragged before Anabetha's court. On the human's pole, the head of Vhalot was balanced, her expression as grim in death as it had been in life. I'd liked her. Despite everything. It gave me no pleasure to see her like that.

But where was Queen Anabetha? Hadn't she returned to the mortal world?

I shivered. Those heads could just as easily be mine or my parents' or my friends'. This needed to end. Now.

I stood up on Rocky's shoulders, nearly losing my balance when out of nowhere he roared. It was like the sound of rocks sliding down a cliff face. That should get their attention.

"Stop!" I called.

Maybe we could still end this bloodlessly. Maybe we could still win this battle. Hope soared through me, sharp and bright.

The roar that answered Rocky swept it away. Down the ranks of humans and fae, an answering roar rose up as swords and polearms were lifted in the air and bloodthirsty screams ripped through every throat. They turned all at once, but not toward each other, away from each other and toward our ring of golems.

No! It wasn't supposed to go like this.

Even my sister and Eckelmeyer stopped their dance. Their eyes met for one terrifying second and then they turned towards me with matching grim smiles on both their faces.

Well, I'd succeeded at one thing. I'd stopped them from fighting each other. The only problem was that now they were united in fighting me.

I swallowed as the earth began to shake under us. A thousand feet moved all at once, charging.

Warcries filled the air as they ran, and the golems met their cries with the rock-cracking sounds of their own calls. Blade met rock as the first warriors reached my army.

The golem nearest us swung an arm like a hammer, driving a human attacker into the earth like a sledgehammer driving a spike. On the other side of us, another golem seized a Fae warrior by the foot, swinging him like a scythe to knock down the other Fae warrior with him.

I tried to see what was going on, but there was just too much to take in at once.

I loosed an arrow toward Sir Eckelemeyer as he charged through the mud toward us, but another human darted in front of him, not noticing my arrow until it plunged through his evil heart. I swallowed and drew again, but they were coming too quickly to stop. With the fluid calm that came over me when I shot, I drew and loosed, drew and loosed until my quiver was empty. But what were five fighters compared to a sea of warriors on every side?

My sister was calling something out, but with the roar of blood in my ears, I couldn't hear it.

I jammed my bow back into the quiver and pulled the needle from my belt with trembling hands as Rocky's fist swung out toward a charging unicorn, smacking it solidly in the skull. The creature stumbled three more steps before collapsing, spilling its riders to the muddy ground.

I had to focus to keep from falling from Rocky's broad shoulders as he dove into the mass of bodies raging toward us. I clung to his craggy forehead with one hand while I lunged and struck with the needle in my other hand.

My breath came quickly, rasping in my lungs as I spun and struck, spun and struck, trying to hit anything that managed to get in under Rocky's wide arm sweeps. There were too many of them. I'd lost track of my sister, lost track of Sir Eckelmeyer, lost track of our own golems and everything else beyond the moment-by-moment conflict I was immersed in.

There was a cheer beside us, and I lifted my eyes long enough to see one of our golems go down. A huge human warrior jumped onto his chest, a metal hammer in his hands. He lifted it above his head and then pain flared along my jaw.

I lost track of the golem as my hand shot up to touch my face. Blood came away from my hand and everything went dark for a moment. I blinked twice before I realized my blindfold had come down. All I was seeing was the echoes of the spirit world and the bright, shining Fae with their glittering spirit trails.

This was a complete disaster.

I'd led my army here thinking we could easily persuade these other armies to drop their arms and surrender. I'd been horribly mistaken and now all I could do was taste bitterness in my mouth as I tried to live second to second.

"Alastra!" my sister's voice cut through the chaos around me.

Rocky slipped and I clung to him as he fought to right himself. We were sliding over mud and trampled bodies. One look at the carnage under his feet made me lean forward and heave up the water I'd drunk that morning.

"Alastra!" I found her gaze across the battlefield, met her glittering, triumphant eyes. "Surrender and your golems will survive!"

But not me. She wasn't bargaining for that.

"You should know when you're beaten!" she cried.

I really should. But I didn't. I never knew when I was beaten.

I swallowed.

Was this it? Was this the end? Was this really all I could do? I reached toward the book in my pocket – the one with Scouvrel's love letter in it – and my hand caught on the cage on my belt. It was so easy to forget when it wasn't being used.

What if ....

I closed my eyes, trying to ignore the feeling of Rocky stumbling under me, of my body hitting the mud, of something dragging me by the braid.

Instead, I thought of all the Fae in the mortal world. I thought of how they'd tried to take it over. I thought of my sister and her claims to greatness. And I thought of how wrong they were. Because even if they killed me here, they were nothing more than petty, squabbling, twisted creatures – like rats fighting over the same garbage heap.

Not rats. Ants. Tiny, small ants.

I felt the cage shift in my grasp, but I held onto that thought, refusing to open my eyes. Refusing to think of anything else until the idea was solid in my mind.

There was a sound like a collective gasp from around me. I wasn't being dragged anymore.

I waited a heartbeat, hoping ...

I exhaled and opened my eyes.

Chapter Sixteen

With my blindfold down, I didn't have to look at what I was lying in, and I was grateful for that as I pushed myself to my feet, trying to ignore the way the mud that my hands pressed into as I gained my feet didn't feel much like mud at all. I swayed for a moment, a dull roar coming from the cage at my side.

The cage had changed. I stared at it, stunned.

Was that even possible? Where there had once been iron bars, there was now a fine iron mesh – so fine that I could see into the cage but even a gnat would not get out of it. Inside, the tiny bodies in a heap that screamed and shook weapons at me were no larger than that gnat.

I swallowed and pulled my blindfold back up at the same moment that a roar sounded from nearby. I was still struggling with it when a huge stone hand lifted me by a leg and it was all I could do to hold onto my needle and blindfold without losing one or the other.

After a moment, I was thrown roughly onto Rocky's shoulder and I groaned with pain as I finished tugging the blindfold back up.

A wave of humans rushed toward us in a charge, their weapons up and eyes wide. I cursed angrily. I was out of arrows. We were surrounded. My heart galloped as I tried to think of some way out of this one.

I saw Rocky make a circle motion with his hands. Beyond the human soldiers, the golems – the ones still whole – began to pick themselves up, circling the warriors. They would be too late. Somehow, Rocky and I had found ourselves in the middle of the clearing. We must have fought our way here without realizing it. And the humans left on the field were all centering around us.

They rushed forward, eyes bright.

There were so few left. I didn't recognize anyone from Skundton. I didn't see Olen, either.

Frantic, I clung to Rocky as he fought, but every time he lunged for an enemy – his huge arms lashing out in punches of stone – I was jarred so hard that I had to use both arms to cling to him. I couldn't get my own stabs in, though I would have liked to.

He pivoted forward and knocked over six attackers at once, using his arm like a bar of rock to knock them from their feet. One of them lay in the mud face down, his head at the wrong angle to his body. I felt a sharp pang of guilt, but we were already spinning as Rocky met another attack, slamming his fist down on one head only to bring it back up and knock a knight right from his charging horse.

It was like something from a legend.

And it wouldn't be enough.

Even as he fought to hold our enemies back, they closed in closer and closer. One slipped in behind Rocky's back and I leaned down to stab with Scouvrel's needle.

Where were the other golems? I looked up as my opponent slumped. The golems were forming a loose circle around the perimeter, reverting to their old orders, but they seemed more intent on making the circle perfect than on actually arriving in time to save us. I made an irritated sound at the back of my throat, but I couldn't spare the energy to ask Rocky to give a new order. One moment spent doing that would be one moment too many. The spot where the warrior had almost hit Rocky's back was filled with two new warriors and as I tried to stab down with my brass needle, they were stabbing up.

Harsh laughter echoed over their heads.

"You're back, wife, and as always, you are causing me trouble!"

Sir Eckelmeyer.

I was pretty sure he was insane. The way his eyes glittered as he said that was almost Fae. Why hadn't anyone killed him yet? He richly deserved it.

I managed a lucky stab through the neck of one of the men fighting me. And gasped with relief. I'd be dead already if Rocky wasn't moving so quickly as he fought. I was a moving target, dodging and weaving unexpectedly and that made me hard to hit.

Eckelmeyer took the place of the man I'd stabbed, quickly and neatly as if he'd planned it. His manic smile made my skin crawl.

"Come down, wife. We haven't had our honeymoon yet."

Being married to two murderous men was one too many. I jabbed at him with my sewing needle sword. He parried it easily with his double-handed blade. I shifted my weight to plunge the needle toward his chest a second time. This time, the heavy blow of his huge sword flicked it from my grip, and it went spinning through the air. Why did that always happen to me with swords? I should stick to the bow!

His hand shot out and grabbed my braid, ripping me from Rocky's back.

I screamed, grabbing his wrist with both my hands and searching the chaos for help, but though the golems were getting closer, they didn't hurry to help us. Rocky went down in a flurry of buffeting shields. They were being used like hammers to drive him into the mud. Just one wouldn't have touched him, but he was overwhelmed by dozens.

This was it. We'd failed.

I swallowed, fighting the feeling of helplessness welling up in me.

Ecklemeyer wrapped his armor-clad sword arm around me, squeezing me against his cold breastplate. The stubble on his chin stank of sweat as it rubbed against my cheek. He leaned in close.

"For the mark your Fae lover put on me, I'll put two on you. For the loss of each on my friends, I will take the lives of two of yours, be they high or low. We'll start with Chanter. I think you like him despite his protests to the contrary."

"I thought he was your Knight," I said through gritted teeth.

"Nothing you've touched is clean. Not even one of my Knights. I will burn everything you've ever handled – and everyone. And then I will burn you. We both know that will end this faerie scourge. It started with you. It will end with you."

I gasped as his sword shot up and sliced the flesh of my ear. I started to scream in pain and then there was a sound – only not a sound. It blocked out every other sound while being completely inaudible – like a silent bell ringing so loudly that it silenced everything else. It was a silent but overwhelming *click*.

The world around us shifted nauseatingly.

And changed.

Everything became tangled and horrifying – from Eckelmeyer, who was suddenly his old, twisted spirit-self, to the humans trying to trample Rocky into what was no longer a mud field but was now a mosaic floor of a ruins covered in crawling, slithering roots. I looked around us as Eckelmeyer's grip loosened slightly from shock.

The Faewald.

I pulled my blindfold down before clutching my wounded ear again. The circle we stood in was Faewald, but the area around it was still the mortal world. In the distance, past the ring of golems, I could see those grisly heads still mounted above the banners.

I paused, realizing what I was looking at. The ring of golems.

They'd formed a perfect stone circle.

Chapter Seventeen

I felt my eyes widen in surprise, but it was nothing compared to the surprise I felt when a blade shot through Eckelmeyer's throat, missing my own by inches.

His eyes went wide and he pawed at his throat for a singe sickening moment. A scream caught in my throat and I froze, not knowing what to do or whether I should even move.

Eckelmeyer dropped to the ground like a sack of rocks and I let the shriek out.

"Oh, I hope you weren't planning on keeping him. Pets always cause a lot of trouble and then you forget to feed them, and they just die."

I spun, one hand still clutching my ear, the other hurrying to pull up one side of my blindfold. Scouvrel stepped onto Sir Eckelmeyer's prone form as if he was a stool placed there to make it easy to look around, rather than the recent victim of violence. He bounced slightly, as if testing to be sure his footing was solid.

"My husband," I whispered.

He was whole and well. His belly wound was gone, leaving only a knotted scar. He'd found a new shirt somewhere but still hadn't bothered to button it. Most of what was left of his trousers were filthy or torn to shreds. Fresh pink scars laced his body where I'd stitched his wounds together just last night.

His wings unfurled around him, dark and smoky and the look he turned on me was equally smoky, full of dark promises and unfettered longings.

"My Conqueror. Pleased to see me?"

"Five."

His smile was wicked as it turned from me to the humans around me.

"I had hoped to take my time killing that creature. I had planned to make him eat his own tongue for the lie of calling himself your husband. I had planned to cut off his hands and burn them in the fire for the crime of touching you. I –"

"And now none of that will be necessary," I interrupted a little breathlessly. "You look well, husband."

"I *am* well." His eyes burned into mine and he took a step forward so that our noses were bare inches apart. His breath was gusting out rapidly like he was running a race, but all he was doing was staring into my eyes. "What a lovely honeymoon present you've brought me, Nightmare. You shouldn't have gone to all the trouble."

"Present?" I asked in a small voice. I'd forgotten the power his presence had over me.

The humans around Scouvrel were frozen, their eyes seemingly mesmerized by his blade and the wriggling tangle of the Faewald floor. A few of them were eyeing the golem ring. But there was no way to squeeze through that perfect stone circle and no way to get out of this circle without one of the golems moving. Their only real choice was to stand still.

"A few hundred humans? All for me? You've outdone yourself. I've heard of stunning bridal gifts before – of a library full of books, a thousand pangolins decked in silver bells, a pair of twin unicorns, but this … oh, my Conqueror, you have outdone them all."

"I received your letters," I said and his eyes flared brightly.

"But those were for if I was dying, Nightmare. Did you have so little faith in me?" He put a finger under my chin and I thought he might kiss me but instead, he just held my chin tilted up for a full beat before smiling at me.

"What happened to my father?" I asked, still trying to catch up. I felt my cheeks heating at Scouvrel's look and I didn't want to admit that I hadn't actually meant to gift him a few hundred people as a wedding gift.

"I'm here."

I turned to see my father behind me, weary-eyed, his hands twitching at his side as if he wanted to do something. His eyes narrowed when he looked at Scouvrel. I sighed with relief.

"You're alive!"

I turned to hug him, and his mouth dropped open. "Allie! Your ear!"

"It's nothing," I said, embracing him.

"It's half gone!"

A snarl rippled from Scouvrel and I pulled out of my hug and turned to him with one hand on my hip. "It's *nothing.*"

"Which one took the ear?" His expression went black as he turned to survey the humans frozen in place. "Arrange yourself in a line. You look awful standing around this place like lost children. Show some self-respect."

I was surprised to see them obeying him, even more surprised to see them beginning to lay down their arms.

"The ear was stolen by the one you killed already," I said sharply. "My other husband."

"Him?" Scouvrel said, looking down at the man dead under his feet. "And to think, I wasted my chance to make him slice his own ears off as payment for this crime."

My response was dry. "We have bigger things to deal with than remembering the slain."

Scouvrel nudged Sir Eckelmeyer with his toe. "If I'd realized how deep the river of his crimes flowed, I'd have found a more excessive way to extract his payment. What say you, you miserable corpse? Shall I divide you up and sell you to the highest bidder a piece at a time?"

"He's dead. I'd say you did an excellent job of exacting your revenge," I said, watching as the mortals lined up, their weapons on the ground at their feet. They were in four lines of roughly fifty, one in front of the other. In the spirit half of my vision, they were nearly as tangled as the Fae. Things were getting worse on our side of the plane. The nervous feeling coming from them was only matched by the nervousness twisting my own belly. What happened now?

"That's the problem," Scouvrel said sourly. "He's dead now and I cannot make him properly pay for the insult of thinking he could marry my bride. He should have been made to suffer for half an eternity."

I sighed and pushed past him. I didn't have time for pouting.

"Is Olen Chanter here somewhere?" I asked as loudly as I could. The blood was dripping hot and wet from my ear. I felt it soak the shoulder of my coat. Maybe I shouldn't be so irritated at Scouvrel for wanting to punish Sir Eckelemeyer.

The mortal men said nothing until Rocky shuffled up behind me, shaking mud from his huge limbs.

"CHANTER. NOW."

One of the men close to me spoke, his gaze never leaving Rocky. "Sir Eckelemeyer left him and a group of others to guard the escape route from town. Sir Eckelmeyer didn't trust his methods."

"Methods?" I prompted.

"Fire. Singing. Sir Eckelmeyer says that's superstitious nonsense."

I grunted. Trust it to Eckelmeyer to say that about the only methods that really worked. I'd have to deal with Olen when we returned to the mortal realm.

"Which of you is in charge here now?" I asked.

There was a long silence until someone in the group pointed at Scouvrel. "Him?"

Scouvrel's chin lifted just a little higher. He had struck a pose, leaning on his sword which was stuck in Sir Eckelmeyer's back, his legs crossed casually and his light shirt gusting in the wind, so that the rippling muscles of his torso were on full display. Of course.

This was terrible for his arrogance. He was going to be insufferable after this. Even more than usual.

I shook my head and drew a long breath.

"In that case, if you don't mind, *my husband*," I said with a tight smile. "Perhaps you could give these men orders to march back down their mountain and go find themselves a new queen and not to ever come back here. They should also free the loyal courtiers and Knights imprisoned beneath the floors of the palace. If any of them are still alive."

"I'll do better than that," Scouvrel said with his most charming smile. He spread his arms magnanimously as if he were bestowing on them a great gift. "I will put a geas on them to do just that and bind them to it. If any one of them fails to obey this order, he will rot from the inside out."

He might have been deceiving them. But if he was, then I couldn't see how.

The look of terror in the eyes of the mortal soldiers was enough to convince me that they believed him.

I took a deep breath and turned to Scouvrel. "I need to return to the Mortal Court and talk to Olen. He needs to settle things in Skundton and to know that the –"

My words cut off abruptly as the cage in my hand began to shake. I cursed. I could already feel the weight pressing down on me. I hadn't noticed it in the excitement of my golems forming a sudden ring and opening the Faewald, but I could feel it now. The price I'd agreed to in bringing my golem army into the Faewald was being demanded. I needed to let this army loose into the Faewald – one for one as I had promised. And I needed to do it now.

"Get them out of here!" I hissed. "Get the mortals back into their court. I can't hold this cage for much longer!"

"Nightmare!" Scouvrel said, taking a shocked step forward.

He reached for me, but there was no time for affection. I ran toward the nearest golem, climbing him like a boulder and leaping over his head into the Faewald before any of them could answer me.

There was no time!

The second my feet hit the ground on the other side of the golem, the Faewald rolled out on every side around me, and the cage burst at the seams, Fae spilling out from it like ants from a hill.

Later in the Faewald ...

B lythe they fought with blood most sweet,
    Hot the battle, hot the war,
They danced with mud coating their feet,
Heavy the guilt that they bore,
They cut and hacked and in crazed attack,
Bright the pain, bright the flash,
Fought to push the enemy back,
Reeked of fire, Reeked of ash,
And who should come but the Knave of hearts?
Glorious, beautiful, deadly, quick.
To witness all the brutal parts,
And render justice, fast and slick.
Forcing peace – now that was a trick!
-Tales of the Faewald

Chapter Eighteen

The cage was broken right down the middle. The bars had burst apart, and the bottom of the cage fell from the top, leaving only the handle in my hand. I dropped it, too. It was ruined. Useless. My greatest weapon against the Fae and it was gone!

I swallowed and looked up. There were so many Fae looking around in stunned shock that they hadn't noticed me yet. But already the Faewald was greeting me, little white flowers bursting out of the ground by my feet. That would give me away if nothing else did.

I fumbled for the axehandle at my belt and drew it with a trembling hand at the same moment that my sister's eyes met mine through the crowd. Her eyes narrowed.

"Sister," she breathed, and murder filled her eyes.

I swiped the axehandle through the air and held it up, hoping the invisibility it lent me would be enough. Hands reached for me and I dodged past a muscular, horned Fae only to nearly be snatched up by a delicate, winged woman with grass-green eyes and perfectly pointed ears. They wanted me dead. Not just so they could steal my role. I could feel the emotions swirling around them – this was personal.

After that, they were nothing more than a tangle of faces and bodies as I ducked and squirmed through them, trying to avoid their blind lunges. They could only see I was there if I accidentally brushed someone, but in this sea of a thousand, there was no way not to do that with every move I made.

It was hopeless. Everything was chaos. There was no chance at all.

I fought on all the same. Allie Hunter was no quitter.

My breath came in quick gasps as I dodged under the belly of a unicorn only to smack right into the back of an orc. I fled, squeezing between two winged Fae who squealed like escaped pigs.

"Grab her! I won't lose her again!"

My sister was right behind me. She must be following me through the chaos in my wake. I needed a way out. Now.

I spun, searching.

The army was starting to scatter. Enough people would cause their own chaos if left alone. If I could just tuck in behind someone larger, maybe I could manage to stay out of reach for long enough that the army would start to spread out enough that I could flee without being touched.

I heard orders being yelled, but the Fae seemed disinclined to listen. They were naturally breaking into groupings that appeared to be different courts.

"Home calls to me," one of them muttered as he passed by. It was like the book said. They were being drawn back into the heart of the Faewald.

One of the Court of Twilight orcs passed close to where I was, and I leapt into the space just behind his back. He held a huge battle axe – worryingly sticky on the edge – over his shoulder and that kept anyone from standing too closely behind him. I crouched slightly to keep my head under the sweep of his axe. It was hard not to lose my nerve as the largest, most imposing warriors joined him to stride through the crowd.

"Whatever magic expelled us from the Mortal World can be untangled and then we'll return," a hulking Fae female said as she joined him. "We'd almost finished with that little Mortal army and I wanted to see the ocean."

"I wanted to try this 'sausage' I heard about," the one I was following said. "It's not really conquering if you don't have a feast afterward.

"But first, we need to check on our holdings here. It will do us no good to lose what we have just to gain mortal charms."

There were murmurs of agreement at that. They were trying to justify the pull that they felt. It really was drawing them back into their own world.

There!

A wide gap opened up beside them and I hurried out from behind the orc, running across the spider-grass of the field while I had the chance, my axe handle torch held high. I didn't need to light my path – the white light of day was bright, and the sky was cloudless – but I needed every second of invisibility as I ran toward the sound of a brook babbling. I needed stones. If stone circles from the mortal world were opening the way to the Faewald, then stone circles here could open the way to the mortal world.

I hurried to the river, dodging a frog as large as a hound, and started to gather rocks to form a circle.

"WHY DO YOU DISTURB ME?" the first one asked. I nearly dropped it. Instead, I swallowed and tried to keep my voice down. I'd almost forgotten that I'd made the Faewald rocks speak!

"Can you please be quiet? I'm trying to form a stone circle!"

"IS IT CIRCLE TIME ALREADY?"

"Gah!" I jammed it into the ground ignoring its muttered protest. This was not helping things! Scouvrel was right. Giving the rocks of the Faewald a voice had come back to bite me.

I didn't look in the brook. I didn't want to see drowned souls or tethered bodies or whatever other horror the Fae had put there. Hurry and anxiety caused sweat to break out across my brow as I fumbled to form a stone ring. It needed to be big enough to step inside, that was all. But the side of the brook was more earth and grass than stone and finding enough stones was proving difficult.

"I DON'T LIKE THIS SPOT."

"SHE IS PUTTING US TOO CLOSE TOGETHER!"

"RINGS ARE FOR FINGERS, NOT FOR STONES!"

I put the axe handle down for a moment as I dug into the bank with both hands. I just needed a few more rocks. There must be some in here. It didn't help that lily pads were springing up around my feet and little pea sprouts around my fingers. The Faewald loved me a bit too much.

Cruel laughter rang out on the grassy riverbank above me.

I froze, my hands muddy, eyes wide.

"Mortals are such low creatures. They scrabble in the dirt when they could be ruling from a heap of skulls."

"Kinslayer." I swallowed hard at the sight of him standing above me, my rusty sword clutched in one hand. With the other, he scooped up my axe handle. I tried not to look upset. If I did, he'd know it was important.

"It's a delightful trinket that you left me, daughter. A sword that takes you to whoever you search for."

"Why look for me at all?" I asked, dropping a muddy stone into the ring. Two more. Just two more. I began to dig in the earth again. There had to be one somewhere.

"Why look for the only kin I know?"

"I thought the Fae couldn't have children and that's why you steal ours," I said snidely. "I'm certainly no daughter of yours."

"Oh, but mortals can bear us sons and daughters. Didn't our tricky Knave tell you that? He can get *you* with child as long as you stay mortal. But perhaps he doesn't plan on watching you live that long."

I froze and he gasped with delight.

"He doesn't plan on letting you live? How delicious. That's a tidbit of drama I will enjoy for a while. But he can't kill you himself. He's one of the four. Just like you. Just like me."

He rubbed his chin like he was thinking as my fingernails scraped across something solid. I dug harder.

"LEAVE ME BE!" the rock complained. "I LIKE IT HERE!"

"Your mother knew, you know, Balance. When I brought her here, the Sooth spoke over her and she knew. She would have two children. Twins. They would be the hope or the doom of the Faewald. I had planned to keep her here and to raise her children, but some fool freed her and let her go and then the circles closed and when next they opened, you were grown."

"I'm not your child," I said, heaving the stone into the circle. One more. Just one more and I would be able to squeeze into that circle.

"Aren't you?" he asked. "Don't you feel a kinship to this place? You even married one of the Fae. It's in your blood. Your violence, your trickery, your little deceptions – it's part of everything you are."

I dug again and broke a fingernail against the rock.

"OW!"

If I could just keep him talking, I could finish the circle and flee.

"So, what now?" I asked. "Do you give me over to my sister? Is she your kin, too?"

"Of course she is," the Kinslayer said. "And yes, I'll likely give you to her in the end, but not until I can think of a good bargain to get for you."

"So all this talk about kin is meaningless."

He laughed. "Of course not. I won't lose you. I'll see you in the Wild Hunt every Blood Moon. We'll ride together you and me. A fitting end. Your mother jilted me. I will kill her offspring – and mine. As the Balance, I would think you'd appreciate that."

"As the Kinslayer, I would think you'd see that I deserve vengeance on you for that," I replied. My rock was almost loose. There! I pulled it free.

"Your sister can get the vengeance if she thinks she can take it." His smile was so wide that he couldn't possibly suspect what I was doing.

And his words told me one thing – he would never stop being a problem for me. This was personal for him.

He snapped my axe handle over his knee so quickly that by the time my mouth fell open in horror, he had already slid the sword into the scabbard and pulled his whip from his belt, excitement in his cat's eyes.

I grabbed the last stone and placed it carefully into the circle.

"DON'T PUT ME THERE!"

The ring complete, it showed a patch of tumbled rock not much larger than I was, but that was all I needed.

The Kinslayer's brow crinkled. "What are –?"

He didn't have time to finish his sentence. I reached out, grabbed his bone necklaces and pulled him as I threw myself backward into the circle.

Chapter Nineteen

A guttural cry met my ears.

I blinked at the yell, looking around me. We were beside the creek that ran close to Skundton. I recognized the half-broken mossy fence on the other side. I gasped and let go of the Kinslayer at the same time that something knocked me to my feet.

The Kinslayer roared and then something like a hammer hitting a wet stump filled my ears and the roar cut off.

I pulled my blindfold up and twisted to look behind me.

My father stood over the Kinslayer, his sides heaving with gasping breaths. In my father's hands was a large, blood-splattered rock. It had caved in the Kinslayer's skull with a single blow.

I turned to the side and retched, wiping my mouth with the back of my hand as I stood shakily.

"Sometimes your mother had nightmares about him in the past few weeks," my father said in a faraway voice. "She would wake up screaming. He stole her when she was just a girl. Not much older than you are, Allie."

I ran a hand through my hair. I felt hot all over.

"For 'immortals', they're surprisingly easy to kill," I said, managing to sound wry despite how shaken I felt inside. "Are you ... are you shaken, Father?"

He looked up from his kill with clear eyes that held a worrying intensity.

"No, Allie. You should know better than that. I taught you that some things need to be killed. Predators. Dangers. Things that can hurt the innocent. Who is this Kinslayer if he isn't that?"

"How did you know it was him this time but not when we rescued Scouvrel from him?"

"Your mother described him in detail. I got the memory back at last."

I shook my head mutely, my gaze drifting back to the Kinslayer dead on the ground. Here in the mortal world, he looked smaller and less intimidating than he had in the Faewald.

"How can I see him?" I asked, experimenting by pulling my blindfold down and up again. "I shouldn't be able to see him with my blindfold on and yet here he is."

"It's circle time," my Father said. "The wall between the worlds is thin. That's why the stone circles can be made anywhere again. My memories are coming back, Allie. I have so much to tell you."

"Why did you never say anything? If you knew ... if you both knew." I felt confused. "That night that Hulanna went missing, you both said that no one had gone through the circle since you were babies, but if mother went through when she was a girl, then that wasn't true."

"We made a vow to each other to pretend it never happened – to push it aside. To never speak of it. It was better to forget."

"Well, that worked out well, didn't it?"

He shook his head. "By the time Hulanna slipped through the circle, the memories had faded. Your mother had convinced herself it hadn't happened at all. We both had."

He dropped the stone beside him and wrenched my sword from the Kinslayer's belt and offered it to me. As our hands met, a white light shot up from him, filling the sky with a bright sigil that looked like a half-full moon. I swallowed hard as I sheathed the sword.

"You're the Kinslayer now," I pointed to the sigil. "You have the role no matter whether you want it or not."

"No, Little Hunter. I'm not going to get tangled up in that world of theirs. Not even if a white light wants to shine above my head." He looked up with a twisted smile before turning its warmth back to me and wrapping me in a hug. "I've been worried about you."

"I was more worried about you. How long have I been gone?"

"A couple of days," my father answered. The expression on his face was grim. "And the next time you go running off, you should warn me. I'm not the one who married that Fae scoundrel and I shouldn't be stuck babysitting him every time you get the itch to go somewhere."

"His name is *Scouvrel*," I corrected.

"I said what I meant," my father said dryly.

"Is he here?" I asked, suddenly feeling warm and flushed.

"No," my father's expression told me he'd seen the eagerness in my eyes.

"But he was here with you before I leapt out of the circle with the cage. We spoke. He killed Sir Eckelemeyer." Now I felt like I was the one with the faulty memory.

"He was. He healed quickly once we went through the circle. I saw the skin knit together before my eyes. A man doesn't forget that." He shook his head. "It was only a matter of finding shelter and guarding the door against insects until he finished healing himself. The Fae are somewhat immortal, though as I just demonstrated, they can be killed if you're bold enough to try."

"Insects?" I asked and my father held his hands apart to indicate a size about as big as my arm.

"Big ones."

"Where did he go?" I asked, not liking how shy my voice sounded. What business was it of his if I was eager to see my own husband?

My father cleared his throat from behind us. "I don't like that you're married, Allie. I like it even less that you married without my approval. And worse than that, you married a Fae and to put the ultimate insult to it, you married *that Fae* who is twisty and deceptive and who thinks far too much of himself."

"You mentioned all that," I said. "And then you saved his life."

He looked at me tenderly. "I will always take care of you, daughter, for as long as you are alive. That's what fathers do."

"And Hulanna?" I felt a stab of pain at mentioning her, but she was still our family.

"You can't make choices for other people. You can't do the right thing for them. You can't drag them into what is good. You can only try. I tried, Allie. I did. And while I like to think that your sister will one day return to her senses ... well, it only hurts when I think about her and I can't do that very often or I'll go crazy again."

I nodded, feeling tears prick my eyes. Our family had reduced by half. My mother was gone – even if it was hard to believe that was even true. And my sister ... my sister had chosen to abandon us when she wasn't torturing us.

I twisted my hands together awkwardly.

"We can talk more on the way," my father said after a long moment of us both staring at the dead Kinslayer. "We need to go and meet the Chanter boy."

"We're meeting Olen?" I asked.

My father nodded. "Whatever your husband's failings, inspiring fear in Queen's soldiers is not one of them. They left the moment the golems opened the circle again and they didn't bother to clear out their things. Olen's men have been gathering up their tents and supplies to restock the town. Your husband sent your army to guard the stone circle on top of the mountain and then he went into the Faewald after you. Fool boy. He tricked me into staying here. Now, I'm on my way to meet Olen at what was once his house in the center of town. And I'm already late."

"He does tend to trick people," I said ruefully. "But it was probably for the best. I know how much you hate the Faewald."

"It took everything I ever loved from me and the only thing it's given back is you."

I couldn't meet his eyes when he said that. I wasn't sure it had given me back. I wasn't sure I'd ever be free of it.

"Dad," I said, putting my hand on his arm. "Everything seems to go from one insane risk to the next and before the waves come and sweep you away from me again, I want you to know that I'm glad to have you back. That I missed you. And that I'm really sorry about Mom."

He wrapped an arm around me in a quick hug, his voice gruff. "I know."

"And if for whatever reason we get split up again, I want to thank you for teaching me everything I needed to know to get through all this insanity. There's nothing more that you need to do for me, Dad."

I wrapped my arm around his shoulders and squeezed, just like he'd done for me. He flinched.

"Are you okay?"

Ruefully, he shook his head and pulled the shoulder of his coat and shirt back so I could see his shoulder. The wound from where my sister had nailed him to the tree was still there.

"It hasn't healed?"

"None of us leaves this life uninjured, daughter. The question is never *if* you will bear wounds. The question is only which wounds you will bear and how well you will endure them."

I swallowed. "At least it's over now."

He gave me a long look before clearing his throat. "Actually, Allie, I think there *is* something I need to do for you. This isn't over yet."

Chapter Twenty

"Walk with me and we can talk," my father said.

I nodded, following him down the path toward Skundton. It was barely recognizable as the path to my home anymore. What had once been a worn trail had been widened and muddied almost beyond recognition. Trees on either side had been slashed down and left where they lay and over everything, strange flowers and mushrooms grew – a little too large and bright for this area. Likely their seeds and spores had been brought by the feet of the Fae. My father was right. Nothing was left without wounds – not even the path to our village.

"I knew your mother all my life," my father said. "She was a beautiful girl. Gentle and kind. A bit prone to daydreams, much like your sister. Ambitious, too. That's a rare combination – gentleness and ambition. She turned up her nose at all of us boys."

"Until she noticed you at the Harvest Archery Festival," I agreed, filling in the details of the story I'd been told all my life.

My father reached up and rubbed the back of his neck awkwardly.

"Or maybe not?" I asked, surprised.

"Well, that's what we told people. There are some things that people don't need to know. Mistakes made. Consequences."

"What kind of mistakes?" I asked in a hollow voice.

"Your sister wasn't the first girl to dance around those stones. And she won't be the last, I'm sure. She sure took after your mother before she became Fae."

I swallowed. "Are you saying my mother danced around those stones, too?"

"She did. And the Fae who came was a dangerous one. He was called Maverick."

"The Kinslayer," I breathed.

"I found her in the woods the next morning. To us in the human world, she hadn't been gone long enough to be missed. Just one night out in the woods. To her, it was much longer. She was upset. Traumatized. I found her crying just inside the tree-line beside the mountain plains. I was up there hunting ghouls for my father. They were trouble that year."

I nodded. I'd done the same at his request before. I knew how tired you could be after a night of ghoul hunting.

"She was so upset she poured out the whole story to me. How she'd fallen in love. How she'd been tricked. How she'd bargained away the lives of her children."

"What?"

He shook his head. "She didn't realize how binding those kinds of promises were. We both thought she was free of that when she escaped."

"The Kinslayer said that the Sooth prophesied that we would die."

My father shrugged. "Your mother said it was a bargain."

"Who did she bargain our lives to?" I asked in a tight voice.

"The one who freed her," my father said, his eyes haunted. "The one she thought she was in love with – the Kinslayer – held her as a prisoner. The things they did! They attended banquets in fancy dress, only to leave spattered in blood, made bargains where she was forced to be caged or endure tortures while others laughed, and other things. Things no person should have to see."

"He said it was only for a single day."

"Who knows what a day is to them?"

I nodded. After all, I'd seen them, too. That just sounded like a normal day in the Faewald. Maverick – the Kinslayer – probably hadn't even realized that she was terrorized by those things. He might have thought they were having a grand time together.

"She made a bargain with the only Fae who would listen to her pleas and he released her – in exchange for her promise that if her children tried to go to the Faewald she would not stop you."

"Ah." Of course. She'd kept that bargain, hadn't she? She'd helped me with advice, but she'd never stopped me.

"She tried to pretend it wasn't true, that it was all a dream." His voice faded to a whisper. "She lost everything because of that promise."

"She did her best," I said, but my words felt like hollow comfort.

"I found her there in the woods and held her in my arms while she cried and then I brought her home and she made me swear secrecy. Only, the next day I was out squirrel hunting and I found her in the woods again, sobbing. I carried her all the way home. The third time, I didn't carry her home. I took her to Fisher's cabin in the woods instead, and I held her in my arms as she cried all night and by the next morning, I swore I'd never leave her again. That I'd hold her all her nights and days. That she wouldn't have to bear this alone. I took her to the Traveler wagon that was stopped just outside our town and I bought her a cure from them – a bracelet to take the memory away. One for me, too. I guess they worked until we were back with the Travelers again. The Harvest Festival was the next day. We were married not long after. I kept that promise, Allie. She didn't have to bear it alone."

"I love you for it," I said. We were close enough to town now to see the stockade walls erected around it, to see the outlying farms that had been burned to the foundations. To see great black scars in the earth and places that had recently been dug up – graves in all likelihood. Many of the trees bore dark stains. And there were heaps of charcoal in strange places. It took me a moment to remember how Olen had been kept in a cage and how I'd witnessed other tortures in this area of the woods. I shuddered as I realized what the char heaps were – humans trying to forget the horrors that had happened here.

"We forgot what the bracelets were even for." I glanced at his wrist, but there was no bracelet and he shook his head before he spoke again. "They're gone now. When you sent us to the Travelers, they knew what they were. They helped us remove them. And all the memories returned to your mother. And after you brought me to the Faewald, they returned for me, too."

"If you hadn't tried to avoid your pain," I said, adjusting my blindfold. It slipped down as I spoke, revealing a town that seemed to be as tangled as the Faewald. I frowned. "Then maybe all this could have been prevented."

"Don't blame her, Allie," my father said in a small voice. "She did all she could."

"I don't blame her," I said, realizing I meant it. "We're all just trying to strike the best bargain we can."

In the distance, people moved in my spirit vision. But what worried me was that they were tangled at the edges, unraveling as badly as any Fae I'd seen. My breath caught and I pulled my blindfold back up, adjusting the knot.

My father's laugh was harsh. "The best things in life are not bargained for. They're given."

"And what is this thing that you think you still need to give me?" I asked him with a tired smile.

"A future," he said simply, but the determination in his eyes worried me. What future did he have planned for me?

Chapter Twenty-One

It turned out that Olen had the town well in hand. Which surprised me, given that the last time I'd seen him he'd been Eckelmeyer's whipping boy.

The guard who met us at the gate led us through the town and my eyes took everything in as he talked on and on, explaining how the local men who had survived had all been under Olen's leadership anyway and so when the Great Battle – that's what they were calling the final confrontation between Fae and Humans – when the Great Battle happened they were off on the flanks singing with bright torches in their hands. While the Fae seemed to be less affected by those things, they still avoided them when they could, leaving Olen's men mostly unharmed by the end of the battle. When Sir Eckelmeyer died and his men fled back down the mountains, the locals had stepped up, gathering the supplies left behind by the missing Fae and fleeing soldiers and beginning to clean out the town.

The magical creatures had been the hardest part. Almost every building in Skundton had been full of will-o-wisps, owl-griffins, phoenix nests, and even unicorn colts. They were invisible to the humans, making them difficult to trap or evict. The guard leaned in like he was sharing a secret when he told us that Sir Chanter was even considering reviving the role of Hunter to try to stamp out the faerie creature populations.

I wasn't surprised. At least a dozen buildings we passed were burned to the ground.

"Phoenix nests," the guard had whispered. And those that were left were nearly unrecognizable. The Fae had left their mark on every one, whether that meant carving human skeletons chained and hanging upside-down along the wall of the bakery as a particularly grisly fresco, or the will-o-wisp lanterns hanging at every street corner that were wrought of human bones, or the way they'd utterly destroyed the smithy and set up a trireme in its place, complete with an orc female masthead throttling a dead stag in each of her fists, tattered sails of fine silk that fluttered in the wind, and a long table within that was covered in shining, delectable food from one end to the other.

I could feel my mouth watering the moment I laid eyes on it and my father's belly rumbled.

"Don't eat it," the guard warned. "It looks so good that you'll want to, but after the first few people made that mistake, the rest of us learned our lesson."

"What happens if you eat it?" I asked. I almost wished I hadn't when he pointed to three people on the far side of the table. I hadn't noticed them before. They were fast asleep, heads resting on the table, food stains around their lips. They had a week's worth of beard growth on their faces.

"It's enchanted. We don't know if they'll wake up. We only know they haven't woken up yet."

He was right. Nothing about the food looked appetizing anymore.

It wasn't only the new trireme or the bakery that was changed. A round wheel, divided into red and white stripes, had been placed on top of a platform in the town square. I shivered when I saw that. Doors on homes had been replaced by Fae doors made of living snakes. The town well had been drained of water and refilled with red wine. Curtains of flowing moss that seemed to be growing longer as I watched them, framed the windows of the town inn and the butcher shop.

"You'll get used to it," the guard assured us. "And we'll get it all back in order. It's just going to take some time."

I appreciated his optimism, but I didn't think that enough time would ever pass to make me think of this as home again.

Along the way, I tugged my blindfold down just enough to catch glimpses of everything and everyone that I could, and the more I saw, the more my heart sank. The mortal world was becoming just as tangled as the Faewald, and so were the mortals in it. I hadn't saved them. Not really. I'd saved them from being conquered by the Fae, but not from being infected by whatever made the Fae the tangled, twisted things they were.

I swallowed down a little burst of fear at the thought.

This wasn't over. Not by a long shot. I'd thought – hoped – that if I "won" my sister, it would save the mortal world. But though my mother had sacrificed herself on my sister's behalf, she hadn't really saved anything. Not if the mortal world was as bad now as the Faewald. And that meant only one thing – that Scouvrel had been right. That if any of us were to be saved, then all of us had to be saved. And that meant I would have to die.

It was a grim thought, and it left me feeling maudlin as we marched through the town that I felt the eyes of the townsfolk skitter away the moment they met mine.

So be it. It was strange to hold your life in your palm and realize you might have to give it up.

I may be willing to die for these people but that didn't mean I had to like it.

By the time we found Olen standing at the East gate of Town, it was almost a relief to see his familiar face. He was a good distraction from my morbid musings.

He didn't look relieved at all.

"Hunter," he nodded at my father. "Allie."

He swallowed awkwardly. "Are you ... ummm ... staying here, Allie."

"No," I said shortly.

I could put him out of his misery and assure him that I'd never live here again, that my ties to this place had been so severed that I had no place left in this town, that I almost certainly had to die to save it and right now the only question was when and whether I could do it without panicking and chickening out.

I could have done that.

But I was irritated that he was treating me like an inconvenience after I'd saved his life and the lives in this town again and again. I didn't want to make this part easy for him. He should be thanking me. He should be hoping I'd stay and keep them all safe. Instead, he watched me like I was that faerie feast. Like I might poison him at any minute.

To think I'd once thought I was in love with this man! He might have lived ten years more than I had, but I was the one who had outgrown him and his small mind.

I narrowed my eyes at him and tried to project Scouvrel's arrogant certainty. *He* wouldn't let someone like Olen Chanter think he was anything but excellent. And neither would I. Not anymore.

"I was going to ask you if you would stay for just a little while, Hunter," Olen addressed my father. "We can find lodging and food for you. I know that you have expressed a desire to leave this place, but we could use your help."

I lifted an eyebrow at my father. Maybe all that talk about leaving this land over that mountain pass had been real. Maybe he really did want to leave Skundton behind. He rubbed the back of his neck again, awkwardly.

"Well, I don't know."

"We have faerie creatures to hunt and no one of experience to hunt them," Olen said earnestly. "We need you. Just for a few days. Just for long enough to help us know what to do."

"That's not what you said to the last Hunter," I said wryly. I couldn't help myself.

Olen coughed uncomfortably, but he didn't look at me. His eyes stayed on my father. Yeah, you never had any courage, Olen. That was always the problem.

"We also think ... or maybe just hope ... that some of our women and children got away from here safely. But we don't know where to start looking. Maybe with your skills at tracking ..."

"The trail would be months old," my father interrupted. "It's too late to track anyone."

"And you don't have to, anyway," I said. Olen still didn't look at me. I rolled my eyes. "I know where the women and children went – and your parents, too, Olen. They must have made it there safely because my mother and father did."

"You know where they are?" he gasped, finally looking at me. My cheeks went hot.

"Well, not the precise location," I admitted, "but I know that they got away and I know how to find them."

There was a yell from down the road and Olen's guard called back but Olen's intense gaze stayed on me. "Where?"

"I took them through a secret portal to an encampment of Travelers."

There was another yell from down the road. "Sir Chanter!"

And then something that sounded like a choked sob echoed faintly from down the trail.

I broke away from his narrowed gaze to look and I felt my eyes widening at the same time that Olen gasped. He took off at a run, armor and all, sprinting down the muddy road toward where one of his men was supporting a pretty woman with long dark hair and a tired expression on her face.

"Heldra!" I heard Olen calling. "You're alive!"

And then Heldra abandoned the guard, breaking into an exhausted run down the road to her husband. When they met, he lifted her up, spinning her around him,

and even from my place at the gate I could hear the happy sounds of love reunited. Even cowardly Olen had a future with someone. I bit my own tongue at the thought, tasting blood.

"Sorry, Allie," my father whispered. "I know you liked the boy."

"That was a long time ago. I don't much like him now," I said. And that was true. I didn't care who Olen loved anymore. In fact, I was happy for him and for Heldra. But it was more than that. There was only one set of arms I wanted to be in, and those arms belonged to the Knave who was in the Faewald searching for me.

I needed to go and find him.

We waited as the lovers kissed and whispered and then as they took their time walking down the road toward town.

"All of them?" Olen was asking as he came into earshot. There were tears in his eyes. "All of them survived?"

"They're a half of a day's journey behind me. Almost every mother and child of Skundton, the elders, the infirm – and more besides. I didn't want to leave the children, but I just didn't know if … if it was safe."

"It's safe, my darling," Olen was telling her. "You're all safe now. I'll keep you that way."

Well, that wasn't a promise he could keep. My gaze sought my father's and I saw that he agreed. It was still circle time. And if my sister realized that – or any of the Fae really, then they'd be right back here causing trouble. More than that, even Heldra's ends were unraveling, tangling together in a grasping, desperate sort of way. If someone didn't find a way to stop that from getting worse, then they would see worse things than Fae. They'd see what kind of evil Tangled Mortals could perform.

This wasn't over. Not by a long shot.

But if I was smart and I went and found a way to hold the Fae back, then this disaster might be over for Skundton. I looked around me and though the place was as foreign to me now as the Faewald was, it was hard not to feel a tiny pang of nostalgia as I realized that I wasn't going to come back here. Whatever happened next, this wasn't my home anymore. And returning here would only bring trouble to these people who I once called friends.

This was goodbye.

"Allie!" Heldra said as she arrived at the gate. She gathered me into a hug. "We're all safe. Thanks to you, we made it."

"Good," I said hugging her back. "And goodbye, Heldra. I have to go now, but I know you'll build this place back into a home again."

"You're leaving again?" she asked me, and I couldn't help but feel insulted at the look of relief in Olen's eyes as he watched me from behind his wife's shoulder.

"I wish you both the best," I told her, kissing her cheek. I reached into my pocket and pulled out the silver mirror, handing it to Olen. "Oh, and this is your mother's. Thank her for me when you return it. She was so very generous to us."

My father was right. None of us leave this world without wounds. And one of mine was the people who never cared about me as much as I cared about them.

Chapter Twenty-Two

I was still thinking about that as I ate a quick breakfast of a bun and an apple that one of the guards had offered me and began my hike up to the stone circle.

"If you could, erm, move your army to another location, that would be very helpful," Olen had said.

It had been all I could do not to roll my eyes. But I did need to go and see them. I had promised to bring them back to the Faewald when this was done. It was time to make good on that promise.

"Hold on to this for me, please," I told my father before I left, handing him the magic book. It was only the size of half my palm now – so small it was almost value-less. Perhaps it would grow for him. Perhaps it had already told me all there was to say. My fate was determined. All that remained was to accept it.

I left my father with Olen and started the long hike up to the stone circle. I didn't look back over my shoulder when I left. Skundton had no hold over me anymore and I had promises to keep.

The broken trees and strange symbols carved into rocks or burned into the grass along the sides of the trail gave me little shivers up and down my spine. The signs of the war and the time the Fae had occupied this land were everywhere. Every time I saw one I tensed up.

Calm down, Allie. The Fae are gone. You brought them out of here in your cage. You're just jumping at shadows. There's nothing here.

But it didn't feel like jumping at shadows. It felt like the calm before the storm. Worse, the woods were oddly quiet. Almost too quiet.

I paused.

Why hadn't I noticed that? Maybe I had good reason to be worried.

Something flipped in my belly and on instinct, I tugged my blindfold off.

Just in time.

A hooded figure leapt onto the path before me. I fumbled for my sword, but she was faster.

Ooof!

Pain flared through me as a blow landed directly under my rib cage, knocking the breath from me. I doubled over, hunching over the pain. I needed to get my sword. I reached for the hilt and a kick slammed into my knuckles, spinning me around. I still hadn't been able to draw in a breath.

Laughter rang out from behind me and then something kicked me from behind and I stumbled forward. Pain flared in my head and I fell, fell, fell into nothing.

I woke to the smell of smoke and pitch. I gagged on it, gasping for a clean breath of air. Around me, low fires burned, their embers barely glowing. Someone had thrown fresh leaves on the fire and the thick white smoke swirled up and sting my eyes. Sage.

"You'd better calm down or you'll smother yourself. The smoke is meant to stop your magic, not to kill you," my sister said. "And won't that be a sad thing? Dying by accident."

"You'd better stop acting like the villain from a story or you'll be smothered by everyone else." My voice was weaker than I would have liked. "Does burning sage really stop magic?"

My sister shrugged. "Who knows? You tell me. Can you feel your access to magic? Can you Balance this out?"

I could not. Even coughing and disoriented, I couldn't feel the pull of being the balance. I let my watering eyes drift to my sister.

My sister blocked my view of everything else, her perfect features painted a bright red on one side and charcoal on the other. I had to blink a few times before my mind recovered enough to know what I was seeing. The sun was setting. That was the glow painting only one side of her face. Judging by how vivid it was, we were in the Faewald.

"You should have killed me while you could," my sister said. "You should have taken over the Faewald with that power you had as the Balance – or you should have made a good bargain with me and been my right-hand woman. Because you've lost those opportunities now. You've lost everything."

The way she said 'everything' with a breathless hitch to her voice made little shivers run down my spine.

"You even slipped up somehow and opened up the Faewald to the human realm. Permanently. All we have to do is make a circle of rocks and we can slip in and out at will – just like I did to snatch you. Do you realize what that means? I'll tell you. It means I don't need to wait to kill you on the Blood Stone at the Dread Door. I can kill you anywhere at any time. Your life means nothing anymore. I can finally achieve everything I ever wanted."

"I used to think that maybe under everything, you could still be redeemed," I said thickly. My head was pounding from where I'd been hit. "That you were a victim first and it caused you to be this way, so maybe you could be rescued."

"I'm a villain, not a victim. And I'm proud of that."

"Maybe you're both."

"Don't move, Allie," she said with a wicked smile as she yanked a chain attached to my right wrist. I tried to fight with my left hand, but it was chained to a wood post beside me. My feet were set on a narrow wooden beam, raised above the ground. "This chain is short." There was a click as she affixed it to a hook above me. "It leads to a stake above. Move your arm and the stake will pull out of the ground."

I tried to move my arm, but her iron grip held it in place.

"Don't even think about it," she hissed. "I won't die with you. Now, listen carefully, if you pull up that stake, it releases a heavy round rock, which will roll out the mermaid's mouth and crush you to nothing but paste. If you fall off the beam, the chain will pull the stake out. If you drop your hand, the chain will pull the stake out. If you breathe too hard, the chain will pull the stake out. So. Do your best. And try to live as long as you can. It's not much of a game if you die right away. We want to see you sweat. And I want to see you die horribly."

She winked at me like this was all a bit of fun.

"Step back from your sister, Hulanna Arnicalla Hunter," an imperial sounding voice said. "And listen to no commands but mine."

Furious resentment painted my sister's face, but she stepped back. It took me a moment to realize why. Her name – which had no power over her as a mortal – had complete power over her as Fae. If I had only realized that before, then I might have saved myself a lot of trouble. I had thought that – like me – her mortal name would have no power.

My hand trembled as I tried to hold my arm above my head without moving it. My head was spinning. It hurt where I'd been bashed in the back of the head. I felt too hot. I wasn't going to last long like this.

Hulanna darted away.

Her eyes met mine, but far from a shared look of understanding, she only radiated more anger. No wonder. Everyone who heard that name had power over her. And now that I could see past her, I realized that was everyone.

We were situated in a black rock ravine. On one end of the ravine was a huge statue carved out of the black rock – half encased in it still. She was a mermaid, I realized, though it was hard to tell from where I stood. Her mouth was a wide black hole and I was positioned on a bowl she held in her hands at chest level, directly under her carved mouth. She seemed to be laughing from my angle and her carved hair tangled out over the rocks of the cliffs behind her, sweeping down to where a river flowed from her navel and into the canyon below. Far down the side of the river, the fins of her tail swept up, changing the course of the river and resulting in a swirling mass of white bubbles.

It was impressive, elaborate, and utterly a waste of effort. Which made it very Fae.

The rocks around the mermaid had been carved into tiers to allow seating. And it was on those tiers that "everyone" stood because those watching numbered in the thousands. Typically, they were cheering and jeering in equal measure. I was starting to realize that for the Fae, every chance to watch pain or death was the event of the season.

Close to the mermaid, in the most elaborate seating tier at the top of the cliffs, stood Anabetha. She was back in that ridiculous dress and armor she had worn as a human queen. I couldn't believe she was getting away with whatever this was. I thought the Faewald would tear her apart as a traitor.

I was wrong.

Hulanna left my bowl and slipped into a dark door that led into the mermaid.

"There has been talk," Anabetha said to the crowd, her voice ringing out in the perfect acoustics of the canyon, "of how I am not truly Fae any longer. Talk of how Hulanna, the Lady of Cups is not really under my power. Talk of how the Balance will come and put me in my place. Some of you are still calling me Malentric, though I have abolished that name. Some of you refuse to bow to me as High Queen of the Faewald." She thought she could be High Queen of the Faewald? How could my sister stomach that? It was her ambition to conquer that role. "I could kill you one by one. I could have Hulanna – who is now my creature – kill each of you in turn. But I think there are easier ways to show you your place and that I am your queen. I'm going to start with the roles. For far too long, our Faewald has been plagued by the roles – by their interference with our power and wills. It's time to end that. Step forward, Scouvrel Knave of Courts."

I gasped.

He was here.

He stepped forward, just like she told him to, but there was something wrong in the way his movements hitched as if he were fighting them. I nearly lunged forward when I saw his face, barely catching myself before I ruined everything with a twitch. He'd been beaten so badly that one eye was closed shut. His hair had been shorn raggedly as if by a knife.

"I know the true name of the Knave," Queen Anabetha announced to the gasps of the crowd. "He must do as I tell him. Take this dagger, Knave."

He took the dagger she offered, a golden handled, beautiful thing.

"Oh, don't look so excited," Queen Anabetha said to the crowd with a wink. "He's my plaything, not yours! But I shall demonstrate my power. Take off your doublet and shirt, Knave. I want what happens next to be clear to all."

Scouvrel froze and Anabetha leaned in and whispered something in his ear. Even from far away, I could see the strain in his actions as he began to undress. Hulanna stepped through the little door and joined Anabetha. Even from here, I could tell her movements were just as restrained and stilted.

"And of course, there's something for you, too, Lady of Cups. Don't think I'm stingy."

Queen Anabetha held out a golden veil to Hulanna. I saw the hesitance in how she took the veil, but I had to close my eyes a moment later and concentrate. Smoke was blowing into my face and I didn't dare cough or sneeze.

"One of the roles – the Balance – is your entertainment for tonight," Queen Anabetha proclaimed. "When she dies, there will be no more Balance because she will die at her own hand, and not at the hand of any other. We will dispense with that role forever."

A cheer erupted from the crowd and I gritted my teeth against their hungry looks and wild eyes. They wanted me to fail. And no wonder, considering the previous Balance had taxed them on everything. No one liked taxes.

I felt a tremor beginning in my legs as my feet began to scream with the difficulty of staying still while balanced on such a narrow perch.

"For the Balance, a game of balance!" Anabetha proclaimed with a laugh.

There had to be a way out of this. Some ally who could save me. Some magic I could call on. But as fast as my mind raced, I couldn't think of anything, and I had to stay constantly in the moment, conscious of every action, every urge to flinch or scratch, every wobble of balance. One false move and I would be crushed to death.

"That's one," Queen Anabetha said. "The Kinslayer is not here, and none in the Faewald knows where he has gone, but he will not hide from me for long. I've already taken his dogs." She pointed below to where the blue spirit-hounds of the Wild Hunt were chained to the rock wall. One of them growled and the other snapped as if on cue. There was a gasp of delight and a few shrieks from the Fae gathered below. They were loving the Spectacle she had made for them. "I will set loose his own hounds to hunt him at the next Blood Moon. And he will find the trap I have laid for him at his home when he goes there to seek refuge – a trap that will force him to die at his own hands. A fitting end, don't you think?"

Well, she was wrong about that. My father was the Kinslayer now, and he wouldn't be going to the home of the former Kinslayer. Scouvrel would be sad, though. If the trap was never sprung, then he'd never get to sneak in there and steal the third book in his trilogy. How would he live on without knowing who married who?

I nearly laughed at the thought. All this fear was making me giddy.

Focus, Allie. Don't waver!

My hand and arm felt like they were on fire. Sweat formed on my brow and began to slowly trickle down my temples, tickling my skin, demanding that I wipe it away. I dare not let that distract me.

"That's two," Queen Anabetha said. "Grab the third, Hulanna Hunter."

My sister disappeared into the darkness behind Anabetha and dragged out the Sooth. She was bedraggled, her hair clipped to her scalp and her face beaten like Scouvrel's. Queen Anabetha was serious. She really did plan to exterminate us all.

"Strangle her with the scarf," Anabetha said in a quiet voice. "Let the voice of the prophet be silenced."

My sister wrapped the golden veil around the Sooth's neck, cinching it tightly and then kicking her feet out from under her. She fell to her knees, clawing at her neck. My sister planted a foot between her shoulder blades and shoved as she pulled back on the scarf. The crowd stayed silent as they watched the horrific pantomime and then the woman who had once been the Sooth slumped forward and Hulanna kicked her over the edge of the tier. She plunged to the canyon floor, tumbling through the air like a leaf in an Autumn wind. By the time she hit the ground the tumult of the crowd drowned out every other sound. Hoots and excited yells filled the air as if the very bloodshed had ignited something in the crowd that made them drunk with excitement.

Above my sister, a bright white light shot into the sky with the sound of something bursting. White sparks tumbled down, forming a stag's head before drifting into the crowd.

She was the Sooth now. She was one of the four. I couldn't kill her, even if I wasn't tied here. Did that make her the fairy godmother now? She would be terrifying in that role.

But there was no triumph in Hulanna's eyes, only terror.

"Hold, Hulanna Arnicalla Hunter. Hold in place. Listen to no orders but my own."

"In a moment," Queen Anabetha said calmly, "The Sooth and the Knave will be disposed of. And then you shall know that I am the High Queen of the Faewald and that none may stand in my way. There will be no Kinslayer to bring ultimate judgment. No Balance to even things out. No Knave to unravel the plans of the mighty. No Sooth to make us tremble in fear for the future. There will only be me and my reign. Forever and ever. World without end."

I swallowed down a spike of fear as the crowd's delight echoed off the canyon walls, reverberating and growing in excitement. I could see why Anabetha had called everyone here. This was her moment of victory and with it, she would seal the wicked hearts of the Faewald to her.

"I shall bring the Mortal Court to crawl at our feet and I shall tangle it up in our woven magic so that we no longer must rely on stone slaves to do our work for us. We will have all the mortal slaves we please."

I twitched at that, and the chain tinkled. My arm was on fire. I could hardly hold it up. I couldn't even feel my fingers anymore. Hold on, Allie. No moving. No twitching.

I swallowed.

There had to be something I could do, if I could just think of what ...

"Hulanna Arnicalla Hunter. Finmark Thorne. Prepare your daggers," Queen Anabetha announced as she handed my sister a matching golden dagger.

A spike of terror shot through me. I tried to suppress it, refusing to react and slip from my perch.

The whole Faewald knew Scouvrel's name now. There would be no escape for him, even if he lived through this. Any one of them could take his will and command him. That realization and anguish crashed over his stony face and echoed in my heart.

"Watch, Faewald, as they obey my commands! Watch and know that I am your Queen!"

It was like an epic ballad gone wrong where instead of slaying the evil Faerie Queen, she took over everything and left behind a trail of blood.

Wait.

A ballad.

A song.

Why hadn't I thought of that sooner?

Anabetha's voice boomed out over the canyon. "Hulanna Arnecalla Hunter. Finmark Thorne. Raise your daggers up! At my command, you will plunge them into your own heart. Wait for it. Wait ..."

I'd never been much of a singer. But I knew that didn't matter. Especially in a canyon where a quiet voice could fill every ear.

I began to sing and my voice naturally found the lullaby my mother used to sing to me.

"Sleep little darling though troubles have come,
Rest from your cares don't hurry, don't run,"

They froze. From Anabetha standing with her arms outstretched as if she were conducting a choir to my husband and sister on either side of her with their daggers held in both hands over their hearts, to the crowd below, they all froze, their eyes glazing over.

"Drowsy eyes drooping from long tired days,
Visions of happy times over them glaze."

I didn't dare stop singing, but what did I do now? I couldn't free myself, and the moment that I stopped singing, they would all go back to what they were doing and Scouvrel ... he'd be dead at his own hand. Just the thought of that sent sick shivers down my spine.

There was no way I could let that happen. I'd just have to sing until I thought of some way to salvage this.

"Sleep in the deep velvet darkness of night,
Sleep in the blinding afternoon light."

If only the Fae could sleep – all of them – forever. But if I was wishing, why not wish for a happy ending while I was at it? There were no happy endings in the Faewald, and there certainly would be none for me.

"Sleep in the morning when blankets are warm,
Sleep, sweet child, sleep and be charmed."

And then Scouvrel twitched.

Oh no! My song wasn't working!

But no one else had moved. Just him.

"Your dreams, may they bring you comfort most soft
So, sleep summer child in cabin or croft."

His arms dropped down and he looked around him – stunned – until his eyes met mine.

"I'll watch over your sleeping form, yes, I will keep you safe and warm,

Oh, I will keep you safe, safe and warm."

He reached behind Queen Anabetha's silhouette and plucked something from the ground. A sword? And then leapt from the rock tier and into the air, his wings unfurling as the sun finally dropped out of sight and the last rays of sunlight faded.

"So, sleep my child, sleep and grow,
Rest your heart, rest your woes,"

He landed on my platform, reaching to unhook my hand from the chain, and in the flickering light of the surrounding fires his haunted eyes burned into mine as I sang.

He smiled, a secret smile meant just for us.

"I'll hold you close, You're safe with me,
My precious bird, my bumblebee."

The moment my hand was unhooked from the chain, he reached out with the golden dagger and slashed the bindings on my other wrist. I toppled from the perch into his arms and he gasped.

"Sleep my sweet, sleep and rest."

He clutched me to him as his other hand slashed with the sword he was holding.

My sword, I realized.

"Lay your head upon my breast, Oh, lay your sweet head on my breast."

"Oh, I will," he said with a wink and stepped through the tear in the world with me in his arms.

Chapter Twenty-Three

"Nightmare, my haunting Nightmare, the terror of my dreams," Scouvrel whispered as he drew me into his hot embrace.

I held him gingerly, afraid to hurt his wounds, but he caught my hand and pressed my palm to his sticky cheek, looking deep into my eyes.

"Delight in seeing me again?"

"Five," I whispered back but I could hardly believe what had just happened.

I stepped back and looked around us. We stood on the Blood Stone right before the Dread Door. My heart began to race and my hands to tremble. Why had the sword brought us here? And how had Scouvrel escaped my singing?

"Truth or lie? You're vulnerable to all the Faewald now. A hunted man. Anyone can bend you to their will."

"Truth," he said and the glower of his one good eye made up for the fact that the other one was swollen shut.

On an impulse, I pulled my blindfold up.

I gasped.

Scouvrel, my Knave, my husband, was less twisted than before, less tangled, the glow inside him less angry looking.

"What happened to you?" I asked.

"Truth or lie? You told me to win you with loyalty and acts of goodness."

"Truth," I gasped. "You weren't affected by my singing because you have been doing good. It's starting to heal your tangled ends."

"Lie," he whispered, his voice husky. "All my good deeds are not enough to save my damned soul."

"But they were enough to save you from my glamor," I said with a smile. For once, I knew something that he didn't.

"Perhaps." This time his grin was boyish and contagious. For a moment, I let myself sink into it. He waited a moment before his grin sank into something far more sober. "Truth or lie? It's working on you, too. Your heart feels more inclined toward me, even though I am horribly disfigured by my enemies."

"I think I like your hair like that."

"You wicked little liar. Tell me something true."

I swallowed, looking instead at the Dread Door. Had he brought me here because now it was time for him to take my life?

He sighed and slashed the sword through the air. "Come, my Conqueror. I did not mean to bring us to this place."

He took my hand in his and the look he gave me when our eyes met was fiery and desirous. He pulled me close and kissed the top of my head and then led me through the rip in the air ... right back to the Dread Door.

I felt my heart sink as I looked around.

"What in the ..."

With an exasperated sound, Scouvrel slashed again and led me, again, through the slash ... and right back to the Dread Door.

His laugh was bitter. "It always comes to this in the end, doesn't it? The last enemy is always death."

I swallowed. "I don't think it's going to let us leave."

He nodded, hanging his head down. When I looked at him – battered and broken – all I saw was the boy who had been snatched from his loving family more than a hundred years ago. Who had suffered at the hands of others and grown twisted with that pain. Who even now was looking at me to save him. I ran a hand awkwardly through my hair and then reached for him, cupping his wounded cheek in my palm.

His gaze met mine and for the first time since I met him, I believed exactly what I saw. The vulnerability and devotion in his gaze were far more powerful than the cynicism and cruelty ever had been. I swallowed back the emotion welling up inside me.

I wanted to give him everything. I wanted to wipe all his tears away and make all his tomorrows happy.

"I'm going to do it," I said in a rush.

It wasn't a surprise, I realized. If I'd really been planning to avoid this, then I would have gone with my father when he offered me an escape. I hadn't gone with him, because I'd always known it would come to this in the end – that I wouldn't say no to him and come here to die.

"I'll kill myself here on the Blood Stone – or I'll walk through the doors like my mother did." It came out in a desperate rush. "I'll let the horror take me if that's what can save you. I'd say I was doing it for everyone – for the Faewald and the mortals beyond the stone circle – but that isn't really true. It's not." I felt a lump forming in my throat and I choked it back. "I'll do it just for you because I want you to have what you begged me for. I want you to be whole. I want all your tomorrows to be full of hope and all your actions to be lit with joy because I ... I love you, Finmark Thorne." Now I really was crying. I tried to blink those traitorous tears away. "And I'll give the last breaths of my lungs, the last beats of my heart, for you. They're all yours anyway."

Searing hope spread across his face, starting in the light that filled his eyes. It was hope and pain mixed into a toxic brew – agony and delight, longing and despair, brokenness and fierce joy. And I felt it with him. I felt it *for* him.

"I thought I could ask that of you, sweet Nightmare," he said, wiping a tear from my eyes with his thumb.

"You don't have to ask. It's already yours." My head whirled with a tangle of emotions and desperation that made me want to savor every single moment I had left. I hadn't meant to fall in love. It was making this harder than it had to be.

"I thought I could take it – to rip from you your mortal life."

"I give it willingly."

"I thought I could bear the agony of your death for the sake of the rest of the innocent children of this world."

"You can."

He bit his lip and then reached out and gripped my chin between his thumb and finger before kissing me as if he was stealing the kisses from my unwilling mouth.

"You horrible Nightmare, you have haunted me until I have lost my mind. I can't bear to let you go."

He kissed me again, making us a tangle of tongues and interlaced fingers and entwined hopes. I was breathless when we broke apart.

"I thought that asking you to give your brief mortal life for all the Faewald was a small thing. What is the sacrifice of sixty years? Seventy if you are lucky? You're nothing more than a spark on a dark night, a mayfly on the wall, a dewdrop at dawn. You're here a moment and then gone forever. Why not give that tiny thing for the sake of so many others?" I was nodding but he shook his head grimly. "I was wrong, my Nightmare. Your short life is more valuable than the thousand years I'll live. Your mother substituted herself for your sister – just like the Sacrifice. Just like I'd hoped she might do for you. But perhaps, it can still be done. I shall take this burden. Nightmare. I shall bear it for you."

He held my key up in front of me. He'd stolen it from me.

"No," I said, swallowing.

He drew a small dagger from his boot – no longer than his longest finger and slid it across his thumb.

"It demands blood," he said with a wink. "Most things do."

He flicked his thumb and let the blood spatter across the stone. The knife clattered on the Blood Stone where it fell.

I felt like I was sinking through the ground. Like it was going to swallow me up. I couldn't speak. My breath was caught in my chest, my tongue too thick in my mouth.

He took a step toward the Dread Door and I could see it all in my mind's eye. I could see him stepping through and never coming back, of me returning to the mortal world free now of the evil of the Fae, but empty and dull without him there. I could see it all.

I pried my tongue loose at the same moment that he jammed the key in the lock.

"Finmark Thorne! You will step back!"

He took a step back.

"What's this treachery, Nightmare?" His eyes glittered with fury.

"You will wait there, Finmark Thorne," I said, my voice trembling. "Until the sacrifice is made."

I leaned down and very deliberately retrieved the knife, standing and cutting my own thumb while my eyes stayed on his.

"Don't do this," he hissed. "Let me. If anyone's life should end, it should be mine."

My blood fell to the ground and the moment it hit the bloodstone, little blue flowers began to bloom there.

"You're not the Oolag, Finmark," I said. "I'm the only one who can do this."

"Then wait! Wait a few more months. Spend them with me. I will show you wonders that will make your hair curl."

I gave him half a smile. "it has to be now. The entire Faewald knows your name. If I don't go through this door right now, we may never make it back here again."

I swallowed and looked down at the knife. Was sprinkling my blood enough, or did I have to plunge this little knife into my chest?

I fell to my knees, swallowing down bursts of fear at what was coming next. If the Fae feared what lurked beyond that door – and they endured all manner of horrors – then shouldn't I fear it, too? Could I handle death? What if it went on and on forever crushing me, drowning me, weighing on me until I couldn't breathe or think?

I was trembling all over now, my hands shaking and dripping blood on the stone. I heard a half-sob and looked up, but it was only me. Only me panicking now that I faced death.

"Release me, Nightmare," Scouvrel said, dark fury in his eyes. "Don't do this."

"It was you who brought me here," I said, choking on my words. "It was you who came and found me in the mortal world while you were working for my sister. You hunted me down and even when I thought I had caught you, it was you who caught me and brought me into the Faewald, wasn't it?"

"Yes," he hissed.

"But even before that, it was you who rescued my mother from Maverick, wasn't it? You, who knew she would bear a child to free the Faewald?"

"Yes."

"You who made her promise not to prevent us from coming to this place."

"Yes."

"You who read the prophecies and realized it took two twins and that my sister was only part of the puzzle."

"Yes."

"You, who married me to keep me close so that you could eventually convince me to die for you."

"I never pretended otherwise."

I swallowed.

"It was you who made me dance to your tune, who manipulated me into confirming our marriage, into absolving you for the sacrifice of my sister, into agreeing finally to sacrifice myself. Wasn't it?"

"Yes," he said, his eyes burning into mine. And this time it was a confession.

"You made me fall in love with you."

"*That*, my Nightmare, you did on your own."

"You pretended to fall in love with me."

"I've never pretended to feel anything for you that I did not feel. You have haunted me to my bones, wracking me with guilt, torturing me with blame, tormenting me with the shame of your impending death. But what could I do? I thought it was the only way to save us all. One pair of girls, given up willingly, to save all the Faewald from our tangled mess. We were mortal once. You've likely seen with your own eyes how your precious mortal town is beginning to twist up with hate and lies – they're becoming as tangled as we are. That's how the Fae started, too."

"How?"

"The thought that you're better than other people is that first thread. And then it grows and twists into hatred and lies, selfishness and indifference. And soon, that twisted mess is all you are. And what can save you from that?"

I stood up and stepped to where he was, plucking the golden key from his hand.

"You said that I can. And I will," I said, glancing at the Dread Door again. My belly flipped inside me. Did I dare step through? How bad must it be if the Wild Hunt dragged people there? What tortures awaited me? Would I be able to endure them? And then ... what happened after that?

I needed to be brave. I needed to feed this, too, to the fire within.

"Free me, Nightmare. Let me help you," Scouvrel pled. "Don't you see how I have earned this death?"

But it was no use. This was my road to walk. I could only walk it alone.

"I love you, Finmark Thorne," I said, barely blinking back tears as I leaned close and kissed his ragged lips goodbye. I wouldn't trade my own happiness for a chance to offer him his.

With a final breath for courage, I stepped toward the door and placed the key in the lock.

Chapter Twenty-Four

"Stop!"

I froze, my eyes clenching shut. Why did he have to make this so hard? It was already hard enough!

"Stop, daughter!" my father's voice commanded me.

I spun to see him standing there in a circle of stones. In his hands, he had my books. In his eyes, concern warred with sadness.

"I read your books," he said quietly. "And all my memories returned. Every one of them. And your mother was right. You had to take me to the Spring of Tears, or everything would go to waste."

"What?" I asked, confused suddenly.

He took a step toward me. He was smiling.

"Do you know why the Kinslayer exists? He exists to dispense justice," he said, showing me the little glowing book I'd left with him. "This book told me that. And what better place to start than here? I read the book your mother left you, Allie. And I read this book of prophecies or wisdom or whatever it is supposed to be. And do you know what I realized? I realized that your mother gave herself for your sister. In her place."

"For all the good it did," I said wryly. "My sister will never appreciate that sacrifice."

His smile was wry. "She has a long life ahead of her, Allie. And "never" is a big word. Perhaps, in time, she will see things differently."

I snorted but that didn't make his smile waver. His face was lit by the eerie light of the Dread Doors, but I wasn't sure I'd ever seen anything more beautiful than his look of hope.

"Perhaps," I agreed, to make him happy. I doubted it. Hulanna had all the chances in the world not to do what she did.

"I understand it all now – how she thought she could save you girls. It had to be you – you were born special, I guess. Together you were one magical being born into two halves. It's weird. I hardly believe it. But your mother did. She thought it could right wrongs and mend wounds. But she never wanted you to die. You only had one mother to die in your place, but there were two of you. She had to choose."

"And she chose Hulanna," I said nodding.

"Because she knew that when my mind was restored, Allie, I'd choose *you*."

"What?" He couldn't mean that, could he?

"She was the Substitute for your sister. But not just anyone could be that Substitute. There has to be blood," he said, cutting his palm on his blade and letting it drip on the rock below. "And it has to be the right blood. My blood for yours, daughter. My death for yours."

I heard Scouvrel gasp from where he was frozen in place.

"Not for you, you slimy Fae," my father said, changing from smiling to frowning in a single second. "I really wish you hadn't married one of them, Allie. And this one is the worst of them all."

Scouvrel's chuckle was wicked. "Your flattery is too much, Hunter. But I can't deny that your speechmaking skills have improved." My father shook his head and Scouvrel turned sober.

"If you do this for her, mortal, then you may call me whatever you like."

"Maybe you could still marry someone else?" My father's voice lifted hopefully.

I shook my head. "I'm not going back on that."

"Just promise me one thing, Allie," my father said, ignoring Scouvrel. "Promise me that you'll take care of yourself after this. No more trying to save the world."

"I can't let you do this for me," I said gently, as my father wrapped his arms around me in a final hug. "Don't do it, Dad."

"It's what fathers are for, Allie. We protect our children. We provide for them. And if what you need is a Substitute, then that is what you shall have. It's why I got my sanity back in the first place, I think." He put a hand awkwardly to my cheek. He'd never been one for acts of affection. "Think of me on a crisp morning when the deer are in the rut and the bucks are out there fighting. Think of me when your arrow flies sure and true."

I felt the tears welling up in my eyes.

"Does it have to be now?" I asked.

"Do we dare wait?" he asked and then his hand fell on mine where I held the key in the door. "If I wait, you'll find some way to take this burden yourself, and I couldn't bear that. Stand back, Allie, my sweet girl."

He pressed the books into my hands and turned the key in the lock. I dropped the books, not even caring that they tumbled across the bloody stone. I tried to grab his hand, but he shook me off.

"Dad, no!" It came out as a choked sob.

He shoved me and I stumbled backward, skinning my knee on the bloodstone. By the time I'd righted myself, light flooded out of the Dread Door, so bright and blinding that I couldn't see.

"Please!" I begged.

My father looked back over his shoulder. "Love you, Allie."

He stepped through and was lost in the light.

The door was thrown open, wider than ever, searing across my vision. Wind lifted me, throwing me backward. I tumbled into something hard.

My heart seized in my chest as light, light, light flowed over me. My eyes were burning, but even when I shut them, it didn't change what I saw. A purple afterimage – that looked a lot like the Sooth's stag – emerged from the bright light, pawing the ground as music – like a choir singing at the top of their lungs – seared across my mind. I couldn't make out the words, but the song swept me up in a flurry of emotion. Hope, glory, anticipation.

Words filled my mind.

STRAIGHTEN WHAT IS TANGLED.

MAKE CROOKED PATHS STRAIGHT.

WASH US ALL.

Was this a vision? It couldn't be real, could it?

Light flowed out from the door, moving as if it were alive.

My breath caught, but my heart was racing as I sped with the living light. We sped across the Dread Door and where there had been tangled skeletons carved there, now there were whole people, alive and beautiful, carved into the door.

But I didn't care about carvings. All I could see, seared across my vision forever, was the last look on my father's face. A look of love. A look of sacrifice.

We sped out across the plains, and the frozen stone statues we found came to life again as we passed. Their gasps of delight followed us.

I wished someone could bring my father back to life like that.

We sped across man-eating plants, and poisonous swamps, and ragged unicorns, and many-teethed creatures. When we left, they were no longer monsters.

We sped across the Faewald and as we bathed the land it began to melt into the mortal world, as if the two worlds were becoming one. I saw the Smoke Falls and my golem army around the stone circle in the same place. Before my eyes, the golems became living flesh, letting out a cheer that pierced my heart with its sweetness.

But even that sweetness couldn't pierce the painful sadness that reverberated through my heart.

We sped down the path that had been lined with wind chimes made of bones, but now they were only chimes made of reeds, tinkling as the light passed. Down further to Skundton, where surprised mortals looked up at us – and as the light touched them, their tangled edges became whole again.

We shot across the Faewald, touching Fae as we went, and when the light touched them all their tangled agony was washed away, making them whole again, right again.

Except for a few.

Because when the light touched my sister, I saw the growl form in her throat and watched as she fought against the touch.

And as the light washed past her, she fell to the ground, asleep, and hard as stone.

She was not the only one to reject the brightness of the light. Not the only one to fall into the depths of enchanted sleep. There were others – both Fae and mortal.

But by the time the light was done, there was not a place in the Faewald or the mortal realm that was not touched. The tall statue of a skeleton in whose eye Scouvrel kept a library, turned into a statue of a living, whole Fae with smiling eyes and rippling wings. The horrific carvings and bone decorations transformed into beauty.

Just watching was enough to wring me out and leave me swaying with exhaustion.

I'd lost my father and my mother.

For this.

"Washed," Scouvrel gasped. Somehow, I had ended up in his arms. "Just like I thought it would be. There will be no more children dragged away by the Fae, Nightmare. There will be no more mortals tortured into insanity. No more horrors come to life."

The bright light was fading, but I still could not see, the light had seared my eyes too hard.

"I believed you could do it, little Hunter, but I didn't dare dream of what else it might mean."

"What else does it mean?" I asked, trying not to panic as my vision remained inaccessible.

"It means the Fae's reign of terror is over. It means peace for all who want it."

"I want it," I sighed. "But things are never so simple. Eventually, people will start to tangle again."

"I have no doubt that when that day comes, you will terrify them all into submission, Nightmare. No one will be safe while you haunt these realms."

"And what about you?" I asked. "Can you bear to leave your utter wickedness behind? Do you feel the lack of it like a missing limb?"

He laughed, low and deep and his laugh still sounded very wicked indeed.

"I think I shall still torture you in small ways and force you to play my little games."

I swallowed and felt his breath on my ear as he whispered.

"Ability to keep a secret?"

"Five," I said.

"I have wanted to be good for a long time. I have longed for any hope of salvation. Who would have thought I would be gifted this by a mortal who hated me?"

"He loved me." My voice was choked.

"He did. And so do I. I will cherish this opportunity to try goodness, my Nightmare. And I will be the very best at it, as I excel at everything. Just watch me, as I make all the world pure and just. Hold your breath in admiration as you watch me wave righteousness like a banner and lift truth like a chalice."

I began to laugh without meaning to.

Only Scouvrel would make turning to the light from utter darkness into a competition – and also claim he was certain to win it.

"Level of arrogance?" I teased.

"Still a five, I'm afraid."

"Chance that I'll be able to cure you of that?"

"One," he breathed, drawing me into his chest and resting his forehead against mine. "But why would you want to? My arrogance excites you. My superiority makes you feel secure. My –"

I cut him off with a kiss. He could brag like that later. For now, I wanted to cling to the one I loved and let that start to fill the hollow spaces in my heart.

Chapter Twenty-Five

If this was a fairy tale, we would have stumbled out into the night to greet all the new marvels surrounding us. There would have been throngs of people cheering at the breaking of the spell that had warped and tainted the Fae for a millennium. Little children would have brought us flowers. I would have transformed into a great beauty wearing a glittering crown with my hair flowing like a golden river down my back. Scouvrel would have transformed into an angel of light with white feathered wings and a bright halo.

But this wasn't a fairy tale, so none of that happened.

Instead, we crawled, exhausted, into a nearby flower, settling into the softness of its petals and curling up in each other's hot, grimy embrace.

"Sleep in my arms, Nightmare, and haunt me from nearby," Scouvrel whispered but he was snoring before I even had the chance to respond.

I sunk into his warmth, reveling in the way his body seemed to perfectly fit mine as we curled around each other in drowsy affection. I could not sleep for many hours. I kept replaying my last conversation with my mother, and then my father, and then my mother again, driving myself to tears and lingering there for long hours.

I'd lost them both so quickly. I couldn't help but wonder if they'd found each other in the light beyond. If there was a world beyond this one where their sacrifices and love would be rewarded with deeper love and deeper dedication.

Whether it had or not, there would be no joining them through the Door. Not now, at least. The light had begun to fade a few minutes after it washed over everything, and then the Dread Door had closed with a boom. And when I walked up to run my hands over the transformed figures in the carved relief on the door, I'd realized that the key was gone, too.

"You've lost all your charms, Nightmare," Scouvrel had said when he realized all my magic items were gone, except the sword. I slashed it through the air, but it did nothing anymore. "And yet, I find you more irresistible than ever. Explain that to me, Conqueror of Kingdoms."

I'd had magic for such a short time, that you wouldn't think I'd feel so empty without it. But maybe I hadn't lost magic completely. After all, I had his arms around me. And there was a magic to that. I had the memories of all that had come before, and a deep certainty in my soul of my father's love for me.

Maybe the best kind of magic was the magic of the ordinary extraordinary things.

Eventually, I sank into sleep and woke to light filling the flower in a rosy blush. Scouvrel was snickering beside me, reading the novel I'd kept for him. His face and chest were healed as if he'd never been beaten and I could see both his eyes again.

"That was in my pocket," I said sleepily.

"Indeed, it was, and pickpocketing you was one of the more delightful experiences of my life."

I hesitated. Good things always came to an end, didn't they? Or at least, they had for me.

"Finmark?" I asked. "Will you leave me now? You stole me for a purpose. You bent me to you like a blacksmith bending iron. But you have no more purpose for me."

"Haven't I?" He lifted a brow. "If you think my plans for you end here, Nightmare, then you have a very limited imagination. I have yet to give you a proper honeymoon, you know. As delightful as our trip to the Kinslayer's dwelling was, it was over far too quickly for a honeymoon."

I gave him a doleful half-smile.

"You do not believe me," he hissed, dropping the book and moving close so he could put a warm palm on each of my hips. "Then let me prove it to you. Bargain with me, one last time."

I felt a thrill go down through me.

"What would you have me bargain?" I asked. "I could give you back your name."

He snickered. "You'd give me something I already have? You can do better than that, Nightmare. My name has already been returned to me. Or did you think I would blithely sit here knowing the whole of the Faewald could order me around like a golem?"

"It doesn't work on you anymore?" I asked, my mouth falling open in surprise.

"A parting gift from your dear father. It seems he liked me more than he admitted," Scouvrel said, running his fingers through his unkempt hair in a way that made me think he liked the feeling of it.

"His sacrifice did that?" I asked with a gasp. "I think if he'd known that, he may have been more hesitant."

"And what if he knew that he was taking away our roles? We are no longer Knave and Balance. Can you not feel it? The constant pull to ruin someone's day has lifted from me. I find I miss it most precisely."

I snorted. "I think you can still ruin people's days if that's what brings you joy, you terrible Fae."

He smiled wickedly. "As the last of the Knaves, I will go down in history as the best of them all."

"What history?" I asked dryly.

"The *Tales of the Faewald*. I have decided to write them myself. No one else can do this place justice."

"Of course," I kept my face impassive. "I can see why you'd want to do that."

"So, what will you offer me, then, my horrible little Nightmare? My wingless fury? My spine's shiver?"

I sat up, cross -egged.

"I shall offer you the one thing you cannot procure for yourself." His grin turned wicked and I cleared my throat before continuing in my most repressive tone. "A roof over your head and food to eat. Considering the Fae disdain for work, I think you'll be grateful to have a wife with actual survival skills."

He waved a hand lightly. "I'll sell copies of my book, *Tales of the Faewald*, to fund my appetites."

"When it's written." I rolled my eyes.

"I'll only sell a few, of course. I'd hate to let it become *common*. Ugh."

I couldn't help it. This time I burst out into laughter.

"Come on, distinguished historian," I said. "I have people to check on."

"People can take care of themselves, Nightmare, but books do not write themselves."

"Why don't you start planning your book while you fly me to the golem army I left at the stone circle."

"Only if you agree to come on my honeymoon afterward."

I laughed and crawled out from under the flower into the piercing day. The sun was golden bright – so unlike the white light of the Faewald – and yet around us were human-sized flowers and butterflies the size of sheep.

Something caught me from behind and I gasped, preparing to fight. But it was only Scouvrel turning me to kiss me and then laughing wickedly as he said, "I have crafted the perfect bargain. I will take you to your golem friends and I will swear to be yours forever – happily and willingly in every circumstance – if you will promise that after you check on your people, you will come on the honeymoon I have planned for us."

"If you have to bargain for this honeymoon," I said dryly, "then I shudder to think what it entails."

His smile was the most wicked thing I'd ever seen. "And so you should, Nightmare. For I shall make you shudder with delight. I will delve into all your secrets and draw out your delight. I will haunt your dreams as you have haunted mine and leave my mark upon your soul as you have scalded the prints of your lips upon mine."

My voice was far more breathless than I would have liked when I answered, "It is agreed."

Chapter Twenty-Six

We found my sister and Anabetha first.

They were not where we left them. Instead, between the Dread Door and the Smoke Waterfall, we found a thick cedar forest and between the trees were hundreds of stone sarcophagi in neat rows. On the lid of each sarcophagus lay a Fae carved completely out of stone – winged, horned, tailed, or almost mortal looking, but all with pointed ears. They were frozen as if asleep.

"Who do you think these are?" I asked, stunned as we stepped into the cedar forest.

"Ceranus," Scouvrel said, pointing at one of the nearby sarcophagi. "Elasaru, Detrini, Maven, Teresara, Ulgrok, Trivenerus."

"You know them all?" I asked in a hushed tone.

"If I had to guess what happened here," Scouvrel said after long moments, "I would guess that these are all the Fae who resisted the washing of the light. They were turned to stone instead. For how long? I could not say."

That was when I found Anabetha. "She even has her crown."

"She thought she could take my will, and now she lies in stone forever. I must confess, I find that fitting. Perhaps a child could be persuaded to paint some appropriate epitaphs on her sarcophagus to remember her by."

"Truth or lie?" I asked. "You're going to keep playing the Knave despite the fact that you no longer hold that role."

"Truth," he said, grinning widely.

And I didn't feel the compulsion to counter him or to balance things out. It felt strange to be without that. As if I was a boat untethered on a river, drifting along and picking up speed. I walked down the long lines of sarcophagi and wondered why we'd been spared but not them. Between Scouvrel and I, we'd certainly done enough wicked things to deserve to lie here forever.

But my father hadn't cared when he stepped through that Door for us. He'd given his life anyway.

I found Hulanna at the very end. I couldn't help myself. I cupped her cheek with one hand.

"She was a terror, Nightmare. She was nearly as horrible as you are," Scouvrel said but that didn't stop a tear from trickling down my face.

Maybe my father was right. Never was a big word. Forever was a long time. Perhaps, set in stone, my sister would find a way back to peace and kindness. Perhaps her story wasn't over yet.

"In my history, I shall write you as the great beauty and her as your dim shadow," Scouvrel said generously.

"Don't you dare!" I held up a finger in front of his face. "I don't care what nonsense you write, husband, but if you write about me, it had better be accurate or I will make you regret it."

His eyes lit with excitement. I rolled mine.

"Truth or lie?" I asked. "You're going to see exactly how far you can push this."

"Truth," he said, grinning widely. "Willingness to play my game with me?"

I hesitated, but eventually, I shook my head affectionately. "Five."

# Later in the Faewald ...

"The greatest of all who bore the title, Knave, was Finmark Thorne, known in the Faewald as Scouvrel. His tricks trapped even the most clever of Fae for his mind was faster and his fingers more fleet. Ladies high and low tried to tempt him with their beauty and wit, but he was a lone shadow, a diving raven, a king among Fae, more glorious and beautiful than any who came before or since."

-Tales of the Faewald

Chapter Twenty-Seven

I had expected to find my golem army still standing in rows around the Stone Circle. I should have realized that the Faewald still wasn't what I expected – even now that it as merged to the mortal world.

We left the Cedar Sarcophagi and made our way to the Smoke Waterfall. I didn't realize I was holding my breath until I let it out slowly when it came into view. Where water would have flowed anywhere else, smoke flowed down the edge of the waterfall, falling from one level to the next like a sleepy smoke snake. I'd feared that we'd lost all the magic of the Faewald, but here, right before me, was evidence that we hadn't lost it yet.

"In here," Scouvrel said as we passed a chunk of rock. He ducked behind the rock.

"This is no time for kissing games," I scolded.

"It's *always* time for kissing games, but that's not why I brought you here," he said smugly. The crack in the rock led into a small, sheltered opening where a forest pool and a small cave were hidden. "Remember when I won this place in a bet with your sister?"

"I don't recall," I said a little breathlessly. Someone – probably Scouvrel – had set up a bed of owl feathers and a large black wardrobe in the cave.

"You're disgustingly sticky with blood and dirt all over you, Nightmare. Every time you cry, I think it's the mud plains in the spring."

I wanted to snap at him for that insult, but in fairness, I really was disgusting.

"Where do you get all the female clothing you keep giving me, Scouvrel?" I asked, trying to distract myself from the idea of bathing with him in that tiny mountain pool.

"Magic," Scouvrel said with a wink, stripping out of his clothing so quickly that I swallowed and looked away. Before I did, I'd caught a glimpse of his skin. All his bruises and scratches were gone. Would they always heal like that, or were these the last remains of the magic of the Faewald?

"Then I guess I'm out of luck this time since the magic has faded." I heard a splash and wicked laughter from the pool.

"You can't get clean on the shore, Nightmare. Shed that coy shyness of yours and come clean your freckled skin."

I could feel my face burning as I stripped down to join him in the pool. I didn't dare make eye contact as I slipped into the cold water. But I had to admit that washing off the blood and grime felt good. I let my braid out and ducked under the water. When I surfaced, he was right there, shoulder deep in the water just like me. He reached for me, and I froze. But he only took hold of the blindfold hanging around my neck. With careful hands, he untied the knot and threw it onto the bank.

"I need that," I said, trying to sound fierce when all I felt was foolish.

"Truth or Lie, Nightmare," he whispered. "You can see me now."

"Truth," I whispered, wondering what he was getting at.

He took a step forward and I could feel his toes on top of mine as our feet sunk into the sandy bottom of the pool. I drew in a shuddering breath, wanting to take a step back, but held in place by the intensity of his gaze. This felt too near. Too inti-mate.

"Willingness to accept that you can see again?

I'd been so distracted by his nearness that I hadn't even no-ticed. I gasped. He was right.

This wasn't just the Faewald anymore. It was the mortal world, too. And there was no way that I should be able to see. And yet – I was.

"Two," I said stubbornly.

"Then maybe I need to show you some things worth see-ing," he said with the most wicked smirk I'd ever seen from him. I barely had time to gasp before he pulled me to him, bit-ing his bottom lip as he regarded me closely, like a puzzle he wanted to solve. He winked and before I could gasp, he began to fulfill his promise – most thoroughly.

When we were completely clean, we found clothing in the wardrobe.

I was going to miss Fae fashion, I realized as I tugged on a pair of soft mulberry leggings sewn with silver dahlias, a pair of high heeled boots with more silver buckles and straps than I thought one pair of boots could contain, a frothy white slip of a shirt sewn from filmy layers of lace, and an ivory doublet with a high, rolled collar and puffs over the shoulders. The col-lar and puffs were picked out in a white fur with small black spots and the doublet was edged in ermine. Even mortal royal-ty didn't dress like this.

When I was fully dressed, Scouvrel looked up from where he was fixing his hair with a pair of tiny golden scissors. How had he made it look so good when it was still practically shaved up one side and yet long and ragged on the top? He looked like a black cat might if it had given itself a haircut. And it looked good enough to make my cheeks flush hot all over again.

"I like how you look with one ear," I said, surprising myself when I realized I'd said that out loud. "It shows the whole world that you are one of a kind."

He winked. "It shows them that I'm willing to take big gambles and I always win."

"Why didn't it ever heal?"

"Because I gave it willingly. And I would do the same again, Nightmare. It was worth far less than what I traded it for."

But he seemed very pleased with himself as we left the cavern. He still hadn't mastered buttons. His fresh white shirt hung wide open, exposing his rippling midsection, under the black brocade doublet he'd chosen. He'd tied my blindfold around his neck with another smirk.

"I've grown fond of it," was his only explanation as he walked past, pinching my waist viciously.

I yelped, but I didn't need explanations. It was enough to have my vision back for good.

It wasn't until we reached the Stone Circle that I realized that my returned vision also meant I'd lost my extra abilities. I felt my face fall as we strode towards what had once been the only door between the mortal world and the Faewald.

"I can't fly anymore," Scouvrel said softly, as if he realized I was coming to grips with my loss. "I still have the wings, but not the magic to fly."

"Is that compassion I'm sensing, husband?" I teased.

His eyes went wide, and his mouth snapped shut.

"Terror at discovering you have it in you?" I asked him after a moment, unable to disguise my own smirk.

"Five," he said and that kept him very quiet until we reached the Stone Circle.

The transformation there was stunning, and even I was moved to silence as we stared at all the activity around us.

The Fae were building.

They'd moved the stones and arranged them into a large foundation and on top of that, stripped trees were being laid as a floor. I'd never seen Fae work before. The sight of it shocked me to stillness. Worse still, I saw smiles and good-natured pats on shoulders as Fae passed each other.

What had happened here?

One of the Fae broke off from the rest and ran toward us and I gasped as I realized what I was seeing.

It was Rocky.

But he was a stone-faced golem no more. Slightly green, with lower incisors that stuck out of his bottom lip, he was every inch a member of the Court of Twilight.

"Rocky?" I asked, stunned.

"Alastru Hunter," he growled. "Your army awaits. We will fight wherever you lead us."

I swallowed, carefully weighing my words.

"Are you building a town here, Rocky?"

"Until you call us to the Feast of Ravens, Mortal Hunter."

I nodded carefully, but I saw there was some emotion just under the surface of his eyes.

"It seems to me," I said slowly, "that my former army may crave peace. That you would like to rebuild new lives like you are building a town here, right next to Skundton where the mortals dwell."

"We have made a bargain with the mortals," Rocky said hesitantly as if he were fearful that I would force him to go back on the bargain.

It was all I could do not to laugh. I would have loved to watch Rocky stride into Skundton and make a bargain with Olen. I could just about imagine how wide Olen's eyes might have been.

"Are you here to return to your mortal town?" Rocky asked, his eyes narrowed with worry.

"No," I said with all the assurance I could muster. "It has no hold on me. And I have no hold on any of you. Go with my blessing and enjoy your freedom, Rocky. I have a honeymoon I'm late for."

And what more fitting end could there be to a story about two sisters who had danced illicitly around a stone circle and been drawn into the machinations of the Faewald than to watch that circle torn down and made into a home for the homeless and a shelter for those who too long lived in fear?

Scouvrel had been right. He'd dared to wash the Faewald clean, no matter what it took to achieve that. And he'd been right.

"Pride in seeing your hopes realized?" I asked him lightly.

"Five," he said, and I could barely look at the way his smile beamed like the sun.

Chapter Twenty-Eight

I had expected that any honeymoon planned by Scouvrel would leave me blushing and stammering. I had expected it would also leave him with twinkling wicked eyes.

And while both those things turned out to be true, what I hadn't expected was that we would find ourselves underwater dismantling a trap.

"I don't understand why the magic is still working here," I said as I watched him fiddling with the mechanism underwater in the Bubblewood.

"I've explained this before, deaf Nightmare," Scouvrel said with his teeth gritted. "The magic of the Faewald still has a hold the deeper into the heart of it you get, and the Bubblewood is practically at the center of the Faewald. The magic here will hold for a few more days before it washes away which means this is our last chance!"

I rolled my eyes as he tried again to reach his hand between the whalebones that surrounded the door into the former Kinslayer's home.

"I also don't understand why he set a mechanical trap instead of something magical."

"Don't waste your time guessing what that loathsome Maverick was thinking. I'm sure it was a thought too small for us to bother with."

"Is that any way to speak about your favorite author?" I asked, but I was distracted. In the sand under the portcullis, someone had written, *THE HUMBLE MAY PASS.* It seemed like a clue.

"I'm my favorite author," Scouvrel said darkly. "Accuracy is your friend, Nightmare. Use it."

I snorted, looking up at the portcullis. If I was not mistaken, there was a counterweight hanging from a chain. This was mortal work, not Fae work at all. But perhaps that was the point. Perhaps this wasn't a trap set by Maverick – the Kinslayer – at all. Perhaps this was the trap Anabetha had referred to – a trap for Fae. And if you wanted to trap Fae, then traps that used mortal craft would work better than something magic that they could dismantle or outsmart. Besides, I couldn't think of a better trap for Fae than this. It tested humility – and neither Maverick nor Scouvrel had any to speak of.

"I have an idea," I said.

"When we danced through the darkness last night and you sunk an arrow into the heart of that delicious hind, I followed your lead, Nightmare. I was shadow to your fire, smoke to your flame, twistedness to your straight shot."

"So I noticed," I said dryly. I was examining the counterweight. There was something odd about it.

"But here in the last bastions of magic, you would do best to follow in *my* footsteps, dance to *my* tune, and drift to *my* current."

I might as well test the theory. Otherwise, we'd be here all day.

I got down on my belly and crawled through the door on my belly across the sand. I waited until I was all the way in to sit up with a smug smile on my face.

"Husband of mine," I cooed. "Were you saying something about who should lead and who should follow?"

He looked up from where he was fiddling, and his eyes widened. "Nightmare. Don't move. The trap might spring at any moment."

"I don't think so," I said with a laugh. "It's designed to make you crawl on your belly through the door. Once you're through, you're safe."

"How could you have known?" He gaped at me.

"Ability to trust in my brains when it comes to puzzles?" I asked, standing up and brushing myself off in the water. It was still a strange sensation to do that.

"Two," he said.

"Desire to get that third book in your trilogy?" I asked.

"Five!" he said, so quickly that I almost didn't finish the question.

"Then I guess I will get to see Scouvrel the Glorious crawl on his belly before me," I joked.

The glower he gave me told me he didn't appreciate the joke at all, but he got down in the sand and crawled toward me.

"Nightmare," he said tightly as he stood up on the other side. "We shall not speak of this again."

I laughed. "If you want my silence, Knave, you'll have to bargain for it."

His frown was priceless. "What would you like from me, vicious Nightmare?"

"The right to go through your histories and edit any parts about me."

He scowled. "Great artists don't need critics."

"Then this great artist will get to hear me tell the tale of how he crawled on his belly to get the last romance novel of the series he was reading," I said dryly.

"Fine," he hissed.

But I could tell he wasn't really angry. His eyes were bright with excitement as we passed into the former home of the Kinslayer and walked to the revolving bookshelf.

"It's here somewhere," he said gleefully and then he turned to me and grinned. "Would you like one last taste of magic, Nightmare."

"I'm pretty sure that you gave me that when we awoke in each others' arms this morning," I said dryly, but though my compliment made his eyes dance with delight, he was still waiting. "Of course, I would."

He snapped his fingers and the bookcase, Scouvrel, and I were instantly transported to a place I knew from the past – the eye of the great statue where Scouvrel's other bookcases and his "art" were stored.

"How did you –" I asked but he pressed a finger to my lips.

"Let it be a last taste of the Faewald, Nightmare. One last reminder of what we lost with everything we gained."

"We're never going to be able to get out of here," I said practically. "You can't fly anymore."

"There's a staircase inside the statue. It's behind the tapestry. Did I not mention that?" he asked innocently.

I opened my mouth to protest but he interrupted me with a searing kiss.

"This is where I will write the Tales of the Faewald and where I made you that award-worthy painting," Scouvrel said with a mischievous glint in his eyes. "Willingness to help me create the best work of art yet?"

"Five," I said with an indulgent smile.

"Good. I always thought babies were a small marvel. Let's see if we can top the ones other people have made."

My mouth dropped open in shock and he took full advantage of my opened lips to press his argument.

But he was right, any child he made would be more beautiful, more troublesome, and more clever than I could even imagine. I couldn't wait to meet that child for myself.

Epilogue

I lifted my foot for a moment, drew a deep breath, and began to dance, whirling and twirling in circles and dips, swaying with the warm breeze and the dandelion fluff that blew around me.

I'd put stones here in a circle a long time ago. So long ago, that I had to clear away the long grass growing over them from time to time when I came here to dance.

"It's a fool's errand," Scouvrel had told me as I left our home to come here. He said the same thing every time I came.

But I still make the journey to this sarcophagus every full moon. And I wipe away dust and leaves from the perfect face carved in stone there – compare the lines on my face to her un-marked one, wonder if her hair would still be a brilliant auburn even as mine is threaded with white. And I weave a wreath of flowers, lay it on my head, let down my braid, and dance.

Because there's always hope.

And despite everything, I still haven't lost hope for my twin sister.

Behind the Scenes:

USA Today bestselling author, Sarah K. L. Wilson loves spinning a yarn and if it paints a magical new world, twists something old into something reborn, or makes your heart pound with excitement ... all the better! Sarah hails from the rocky Canadian Shield in Northern Ontario – learning patience and tenacity from the long months of icy cold – where she lives with her husband and two small boys. You might find her building fires in her woodstove and wishing she had a dragon handy to light them for her

Sarah would like to thank **Julie Thomas** and **Eugenia Kollia** for their incredible work in beta reading and proofreading this book. Without their big hearts and passion for stories, this book would not be the same.

Sarah has the deepest regard for the talent of her phenomenal artist Luciano Fleitas who created the gorgeous cover art that accompanies this book. Without his work, it would be so much harder to show off this story the way it deserves!

Thanks also to the Noble Order of Female Fantasy Authors who keep me sane – sort of. And for my beloved husband, Cale and sons Neville and Leif who are endlessly patient as I talk to them about bookish passions.

www.sarahklwilson.com[1]

Follow Sarah to keep up with fun updates:

INSTAGRAM[2]

---

1. https://www.sarahklwilson.com/bridge-of-legends

<u>FACEBOOK</u>[3]
<u>AMAZON</u>[4]
<u>NEWSLETTER</u>[5]

---

2.   https://www.instagram.com/sarahklwilson

3.   http://www.facebook.com/sarahklwilson

4.   https://www.amazon.com/-/e/B0064MSJRE

5.   https://www.subscribepage.com/brandawareness